ROB STEVENS

ANDERSEN PRESS

First published in 2018 by
Andersen Press Limited
20 Vauxhall Bridge Road
London SW1V 2SA
www.andersenpress.co.uk

2 4 6 8 10 9 7 5 3 1

British Library Cataloguing in Publication Data available.

ISBN 978 1 78344 657 5

Typeset by Palimpsest Book Production Limited, Falkirk, Stirlingshire
Printed and bound in Great Britain by Clays Limited, Bungay, Suffolk, NR35 1ED

For my family

MATCH DAY

You know that feeling when you realise everything's out of control? That sort of sickly sensation that tells you the game is up? That awful regret as you look back at a chain of events that took you from being a normal kid to one who's, say, wanted for a bank job?

That.

Alarm bells started to ring when I came downstairs and saw a policeman just inside the kitchen doorway. He was holding up his hands like they do in films when they're persuading the bad guy not to shoot. I took off my headphones and watched from the hall.

'Place the weapon on the counter and put your hands on your head,' said the policeman.

Nobody moved.

'I won't ask again, miss,' the policeman said sternly. 'I said put your weapon down.'

My sister, Olivia, glanced over her shoulder at the young officer. 'Me?' she said. She was gripping a French loaf in two hands like it was a baseball bat. 'He's the one with the knife.'

Olivia was confronting a stocky boy who was backed up against the Italian marble work surface. He was holding a small butter knife, a blob of Lurpak balanced on its rounded blade. His other hand was gripping a triangle of toast.

Reluctantly Olivia lowered the bread and placed it on the worktop.

The policeman's Adam's apple bobbed in his skinny throat. 'Now step away from the baguette.'

My sister took a step backwards. 'It's not a baguette,' she mumbled. 'It's a *ficelle*, actually.'

'You too, sonny,' said the policeman. 'It's time to throw in the towel.'

The boy frowned. 'What towel?'

'He means put your knife down,' Olivia explained.

'Oh right.' The boy licked the blade clean and placed it on a plate behind him.

The policeman's top lip was glistening. 'Right, can someone explain what's going on?' he asked.

'Isn't it obvious?' my sister said. 'This kid is an intruder. He's broken in. I just arrived home and found him robbing us.'

2

'It looks to me like he's making toast,' said the officer.

'Whatever,' said Olivia. 'In *our* kitchen. I'm sure after he'd finished his toast he was going to ransack the house. These criminals can be very cocky, you know.'

'Is that so?' said the policeman. 'Met lots of criminals, have you, miss?'

I knew it was time to speak up – time to stop that runaway train in its tracks.

'Come to think of it...' The PC was studying the kid. 'You do fit the description of one of the two juveniles who tried to hold up the Lloyds Bank on Market Street yesterday. You haven't got a shorter, slimmer friend by any chance, have you?'

Instinctively I stood on tiptoes and puffed out my cheeks. Maybe it wasn't the time to pipe up after all. The boy noticed me and gave me a questioning look. I shook my head slightly. It was a gesture that meant, 'Say nothing'. It meant, 'I'll sort all this out but for now the best thing would be to keep shtum.' It meant, 'Whatever happens we mustn't admit to knowing each other.'

On reflection, it was probably too much to convey with a small head movement because the kid said, 'This is all a big misunderstanding. Tell them, Leon.'

The policeman and my sister turned to look at me.

'Le-on?' she said suspiciously.

'Leon,' the officer repeated gleefully. 'Can you confirm

3

your whereabouts yesterday afternoon, between approximately 4.32 and 4.44 p.m.?'

As I stood there contemplating the mess I was in I
thought back to where it had all started to unravel. How
had I allowed things to get this far?

I swallowed and tried to smile brightly. 'This is a funny
story.'

I

It all started on Friday. My marker pen squeaked as I crossed out the date on my England rugby calendar. Eleven months and twenty-eight days since that day. I realised I was humming the song again – 'He Ain't Heavy, He's My Brother' by an old group called The Hollies, one of my mum's favourite songs.

'Did you hear me, Leon Copeman?' Mum called up the stairs. 'I asked you a question.'

I considered the likely options – took a punt. 'Yes please.'

'I asked if you want toast or cereal.'

'Oh.' Nearly a year since that day.

'Well?'

'I'm coming – I mean cereal please.' I dropped the pen and it swung next to the calendar on a piece of frayed twine. Levering my weight onto the banister I vaulted down the stairs in two bounds.

Our kitchen is like something from a glossy magazine. All Italian marble and shiny cabinets. Dad was sitting at the Nordic pine table watching Sky News. He was wearing a navy suit and eating marmalade on toast. He'd shaved and his hair was neatly parted and he smelled of fresh cologne and Colgate. My mother was perched at the breakfast bar, eating a bowl of Weetabix and staring at her laptop. Anyone would have thought they were a normal, happy couple.

'Morning, whizz kid,' Dad said cheerfully. He calls me that because I'm a pretty fast runner – second fastest in my year. Actually, I'm the fastest now. I have been since … well, for nearly a year. I raised a hand and smiled, sliding into a chair and reaching for the milk.

A charity commercial about the plight of polar bears came on the TV. It said they'll be extinct soon because the ice caps are melting.

'Quick, Susan, change the channel before Leon decides to rescue a stray bear and adopt it as a pet.'

'Very funny,' I said.

Dad shook his head. 'You won't think it's so funny when Snowball eats next door's spaniel.'

'I could keep it in my room,' I said, acting excited.

'Have you thought this through?' Dad took a swig of black coffee and stood. 'Think of the awful mess – the *smell.*' He gave me a serious frown. 'No bear should have to live in those conditions.'

'You're actually hilarious, Dad.' I wished he could be like this all the time – normal, like he used to be. 'Anyway, I don't always bring strays home.'

'What about that three-legged cat?' Mum said without looking up.

'Tripod was cute though.'

'And that bird with the broken wing,' said Dad.

I smiled. 'It's not like Dodo was going to take over the house.'

'No,' said Mum, 'but that tramp you brought home from the bus station might have done.'

'I still can't believe you turned Mr Cheeseman away.' I shook my head disappointedly.

'We gave him dinner,' Mum sighed.

'Yeah, and then kicked him out. We could at least have let him stay the night.'

'What if he'd turned out to be a kidnapper, or an escaped convict or a ...'

Dad gasped theatrically. 'Or even worse ... a Kestrels fan?'

'So if you'd known for sure he wasn't a kidnapper or an escaped convict or a Kestrels fan, you'd have let him stay?'

'Yeah. Sure, right, Susan?'

'Don't try and make me feel guilty, Leon,' Mum said. 'I do plenty to help the community thank you very much.'

Dad looked at me and raised his eyebrows – like, *you can say that again*. Then he got up and put his cup into the sink. 'I'm going to miss my train if I don't skedaddle – see you about eightish.'

'What about golf?' I said.

'What golf?'

'You said we could go up the driving range tonight.'

'When did I say that?'

'When you came home from work the other day.'

'I'm sorry, Leon.' Dad bent and squeezed my shoulder. 'It must have slipped my mind. I've got this meeting arranged now – I can't change it. It's really important. Maybe Mum can take you?'

I looked hopefully at her but she didn't react.

'Can you, Mum?'

'What's that?

'Take me to the driving range after school?'

'Not tonight, sweetheart. I've arranged to talk to some residents of Applewood Lane about speed bumps.' Mum was the founder and chairperson for a local road-safety group. She spent all day every day surveying traffic speeds and campaigning for tighter limits at hotspots. 'Couldn't your dad change his meeting?'

'I'm afraid not, Leon. Mr Schultz is flying in from Frankfurt specially. Maybe Mum could meet the residents another time?'

'Tell Dad I've had this meeting planned for weeks.'

I shifted uncomfortably and looked at my dad. 'Mum's had this meeting—'

'Planned for weeks, yes I heard.' Smiling at me, he muttered, 'The trouble is that Mum seems to think her road-safety crusade is more important than everything else.'

Mum's head slowly rose from behind her laptop – like the T. rex in *Jurassic World*. There was a rattling growl from the back of her throat before she spoke – or maybe I just imagined that part. 'Perhaps you could ask Dad why he thinks his meeting with Mr Schultz is more important than trying to save lives on our roads?'

Mum and Dad did this a lot. All the time in fact. Instead of actually speaking to each other, they just argued through me. It was like they were from different countries and I was a UN translator.

Mum was glaring at me and I wasn't sure if she expected me to pass the glare on to Dad for her.

Instead I studied my juice. Dad sighed and picked up his briefcase. 'We'll go some time soon, Leon, I promise. Is that a deal?'

'Sure. That's a deal.' I'll add it to the list, I thought.

9

'I'll bring Snowball, too,' Dad offered. 'I heard polar bears love golf almost as much as roller-skating.'

'Since when do polar bears like roller-skating?' I laughed.

'Everyone knows polar bears love roller-skating.' Dad paused at the doorway and shook his head disappointedly. 'Honestly, young man, if you're serious about adopting a polar bear, you've got an awful lot of reading up to do.'

He closed the door behind him and I smiled to myself as I tipped more Rice Krispies into my bowl.

Mum went to the bottom of the stairs and shouted, 'Olivia Copeman, you're going to be late for college!'

'All right, no need to shout – I'm not deaf,' my sister moaned, trotting down the stairs, all tight jeans and big hair. Like *massive*. Lenny used to say it looked like she'd been in an explosion in a hairspray factory.

'I've been calling you for the last half hour.'

'I know.' Olivia rolled her eyes at me. 'Like I said, I'm not deaf.'

'What have you been doing up there all this time?'

'Er, he-llo?' My sister pointed a finger at her hair. 'A masterpiece like this doesn't just happen on its own you know.'

'I imagine not,' Mum mumbled.

'What do you think, Leon?'

It was way too crazy. Too wild.

10

'Looks cool,' I said.

'Ah thanks.' My sister winked at me and I smiled.

Mum swept her eyes over Olivia's big hair then over her elaborate make-up – bright blue and pink eye shadow and thick purple lips. 'That's quite a lot of effort to go to for college.'

'I'm a fashion student, Mum,' Olivia said wearily. 'If you're in fashion, you have to be *in fashion*.'

'I see,' Mum said, but her expression said the opposite. 'I have to go. I've got a meeting with the council about cars speeding on Bryant Way. We clocked three cars doing sixty-plus on one morning this week – right past the Little Stars nursery. If the kids had been coming out at the time, well – it doesn't bear thinking about.' She shrugged on her coat. 'Put your dishes in the dishwasher before you leave.'

'Sir, yes, sir,' Olivia said in a gruff American voice, saluting smartly. Mum gave her a withering smile, and a kiss. Then she came over to me, bent and kissed my cheek. Nodding at the window, she said, 'Looks like it rained last night.'

I nodded.

'If the ground's damp it'll be slippery.'

'Uh-huh.'

'Cars take twice as long to stop in wet weather.'

'I know.'

'If there's mist over Chambers Park it sometimes drifts onto the road so visibility could be poor – make sure you wear your hi-vis vest.'

'I will.'

'You need to leave soon,' she said. 'You don't want to end up hurrying.'

'Yeah, I know,' I snapped. 'I'm not a kid you know.' I'd sounded more annoyed than I'd meant to. More quietly I continued, 'I mean, *technically*, I am actually a kid. But I am a kid who knows what time to leave for school.'

Mum's eyes met mine and she nodded. 'OK. But be *careful*.' She grabbed her bag and left.

'Why does she always say that?' I muttered into my bowl.

'Sorry?' Olivia asked, stirring honey into natural yoghurt.

'*Be careful*,' I said mimicking Mum, although I made her sound more naggy than she'd actually sounded. 'What's that supposed to mean?'

'Hmm. What could that cryptic message possibly mean?' Olivia tapped her spoon on her chin.

'It's like she's saying that I'm not normally careful. If she thought I was careful she wouldn't have to tell me to be careful every single day. And why does she always go on about me not hurrying? It's like she's saying *we all remember what happened when you were hurrying*. As if I could forget.'

'You're right. That's exactly what she's saying. Unless...' Olivia paused, holding up her spoon. 'This might sound crazy but maybe she's just saying, "I love you and want you to stay safe"? What do you think? Too weird? You're probably right. Best stick with your ominous blame-laden subtext.'

'Maybe,' I said, but I what was actually thinking was *you're so wrong*.

As if reading my thoughts, Olivia said, 'Seriously, Leon – suggesting you're not careful enough would be like saying Einstein's not clever enough, or there aren't enough cat videos on Facebook, or Blake Lively isn't pretty enough.'

I didn't know who Blake Lively was but I wanted to join in so I said, 'Or like saying Owen Ritchie's kicking isn't accurate enough?'

'Yeah. Maybe. Look, I don't know who Ian Ritchie is. Sorry.'

'Owen. He's a rugby player,' I said, wishing I'd spoken up about Blake Lively. 'He played in the match we all went to last year. He scored the winning try.'

'Sure,' Olivia said, sliding her bowl onto the worktop. 'Let's go or we'll be late.'

I got up and put both of our bowls into the dishwasher as Olivia teased her hair in front of the mirror. We grabbed our bags – a rucksack for me and a large art folder for her – and left the house. At the end of our drive we stopped.

When Olivia said, 'Later, dude,' I got this weird mental image. I saw her going off to uni and leaving me at home in a huge empty house. It was depressing and scary and something must have shown in my face because she stepped towards me and hugged me tight.

'Do you think Mum and Dad are going to be OK?' I mumbled.

After a long pause Olivia said, 'Of course they are.'

I didn't want to let go but eventually Olivia let her arms drop. I watched her walk away then I headed off in the other direction.

2

It was a dank morning and the air was cold. I pulled the sleeves of my jumper over my hands, wishing I'd worn my coat. I came to a stop and pressed the button on the zebra crossing *adjacent* to Chambers Park. That's how it was described in the local newspaper article the day after the accident. I remember pretty much the whole article word for word – along with the headline,

TWIN BOY, 12, KILLED PLAYING CHASE AT ZEBRA CROSSING

I wondered if journalists ever stop and think about bereaved relatives reading their stories the day after. Probably not. If they did, they wouldn't use phrases like, 'Crushed against the safety barrier', or 'Massive head injuries'.

Loads of people were quoted saying how sad they were, like our headmaster and Lenny's PE teacher.

The local vicar said he was going to miss Lenny's eager face at Sunday school, which was odd because Lenny hardly ever went to Sunday school. Everyone said how well behaved he was – and clever, but it was rubbish. Lenny was always in detention and struggled at school to be honest. It was like they'd all been given the same script.

Nobody said he had the best imagination in the world, or that he could do a back flip from a standing start or tell rude jokes nonstop for hours. No one mentioned that he was never ever grumpy. Ever. Even on a rainy Monday morning. Even then he'd been happy. Even then he'd been trying to cheer up his grumpy brother by suggesting games they could play – like chase.

I waited for the red man to change to green. The road was quiet. A couple of kids from my school brushed past me as they dashed across the road. As I watched them run off laughing, I imagined them mocking my fluorescent tabard.

Finally, the green man lit up, beeping. I checked both ways and stepped into the road. My pace quickened, I reached the opposite kerb and released the air from my lungs. I walked on without lifting my head because I didn't want to look at the safety barrier and remember it buckled out of shape.

I got to school just as the bell went. Kids swarmed towards the building and funnelled through the double doors where there was the usual crush of bodies, everyone protecting themselves with bags and elbows. I went with the flow, pressed tightly amongst the throng. The crowd began to disperse as kids filtered off into their classrooms.

My class was near the end of the corridor so the scrum was over by the time I got there.

'All right, Leon,' said Tom Hubbard as I entered.

'Hi, Tom.'

'Coming to watch the game tonight?'

'I can't.' I made a disappointed face. 'I promised my dad I'd go with him to the driving range so...'

The truth was I couldn't bear to watch the school rugby team play – even in the cup semifinal. Lenny and I used to play in the team together. He was scrum half and captain and I played on the wing. He had lightning hands and I was pretty quick too.

Since Lenny died Mum wouldn't let me play because it was too dangerous. She read somewhere that over a thousand people suffer head injuries playing rugby every year so that was the end of that. She even wrote a letter to the school stating that I was not to engage in any kind of contact sport – or a whole load of other what she called 'risky activities'. Now, when other kids were doing cool experiments with Bunsen burners I got to study the periodic table on my own. Awesome.

Tom was the rugby captain now. He was OK but he wasn't Lenny. Lenny didn't make a big deal of being the captain. He just encouraged everyone during the games and got on with it. Tom preferred to start psyching everyone up for about a fortnight before every match.

'It's a big match tonight.'

'Yeah – you said,' said Ash Morton. He was the hooker in the school team.

'Semifinal,' Tom said meaningfully.

'We know, Tom.'

'If we win, we'll be in the final.'

Ash glanced at me, rolled his eyes. 'So *that's* what "semifinal" means?'

Tom nodded earnestly and said, 'Games don't come any bigger than a semifinal.'

'Apart from a final,' I suggested.

'What?'

'I was just thinking a final is probably a bigger game than a semi, wouldn't you say?'

'Sure. That goes without saying.'

'So what we're saying,' said Ash, 'is that, apart from a final, games don't come any bigger than a semifinal?'

'Uhh...Sure. Obviously.'

Ash smiled mischievously. 'What about the last game of the season between the teams placed first and second in the league if they're tied on points?'

'Sorry?'

'Wouldn't you say that match would be bigger than a semifinal?'

'I don't know. Maybe. I guess,' Tom replied.

'So what you meant was, apart from a final and an end-of-season league decider, games don't come any bigger than a semifinal?'

'Sure. I think,' Tom said, irritated. 'All I'm saying is we'll need a hundred-and-ten-per cent effort tonight.'

I desperately wanted to tell him it's impossible to get more than one hundred per cent. Instead I nodded, avoiding Ash's eyes.

Mr Rooney came into the class so I took my seat and bent down to get some books out of my bag. When I sat up again I noticed a boy was standing next to the teacher at the front of the class.

The kid was a fair bit taller than me, pretty solid-looking with fleshy features and pale skin. His brown eyes darted about as though he was searching for something. Half the class hadn't seen Mr Rooney enter and were still talking or messing about.

'OK, everyone.' Mr Rooney's deep Scottish drawl was always full of scorn. 'Sit down and settle down, you're like a bunch of squawking mother hens. That includes you, Simpson. I know you're all excited because today's your last day of school before the half-term break but there's a whole day of learning to get through first.'

Eventually the chatter died away and the class was silent.

'Thank you so much.' Mr Rooney's grin reminded me of a crocodile baring its teeth. 'That wasn't so difficult now, was it? Before we get started today I want to introduce you all to Arnold. He'll be joining the school after the holiday but he's come in today to have a wee look-see. I want you all to make him feel extremely welcome.' Mr Rooney paused then turned to Arnold. 'Och, I know that some of them look pretty unpleasant, Arnold, but looks can be deceiving. Once you get to know them you'll realise that actually every single one of them is pretty unpleasant.'

He winked at Arnold, who just frowned.

'Would you like to introduce yourself to the class?'

Arnold shrugged and Mr Rooney took a step back.

Arnold cleared his throat. 'My name is Arnold,' he said slowly.

Some of the class nodded. Everyone waited. Arnold turned expectantly to Mr Rooney who took a step forward.

'Well, that was certainly a little more *succinct* than I'd anticipated,' Mr Rooney said dryly. 'Always leave them wanting more, eh, Arnold? OK then, let's see where we can put you. Ah yes, there's a seat next to Callum with your name on it.'

Arnold walked across the classroom and stood in front of the empty chair, peering at it.

'I can't see my name,' he said.

'Sorry?' said Mr Rooney, who had already started writing something on the whiteboard.

'You said this chair had my name on it,' Arnold said. 'But it doesn't.'

Stifled laughter rippled around the room.

'I see we have something of a comedian in our ranks?' said Mr Rooney, forcing his lips into a smile. 'I just meant for you to take that chair.'

Arnold picked up the chair. 'Where to?'

'I'm sorry?'

'Where shall I take the chair to?'

A bigger wave of laughter this time.

'Are you trying to be funny, young man?'

'No, sir.'

'Then kindly put the chair behind the desk then sit on it.'

Everyone watched Arnold tuck in the chair. Then the room exploded with laughter as he dropped his school bag and slid his backside onto the desk, swinging his legs.

'On the chair, Arnold,' Mr Rooney boomed. 'When I said put the chair behind the desk and sit on *it*, the *it* referred to the chair, not the desk.'

21

'Oh, right. Sorry.' Arnold slid off the desk and walked round it, pulled out the chair and sat down.

'Finally,' said Mr Rooney with his crocodile smile. 'I didn't expect that to be quite such a struggle. Now, Callum, I want you to chaperone Arnold for the day – be his tour guide, if you will.'

'Do I have to?' Callum groaned.

'Well, if that doesn't make you feel welcome, Arnold, I don't know what will.'

Everyone in the room was smiling.

Everyone that is, except Arnold.

3

Ash and Tom weren't around at lunchtime because the rugby team was having a meeting to talk tactics for the big match that evening. I was idly watching a mass kick about in the playground when the ball came my way. I couldn't resist chipping it back towards one of the goals. It was only a gentle kick but Mrs Richards saw. She gave a long blow on her whistle like a lifeguard who's spotted kids bombing in the swimming lane and everyone stopped to look.

'No contact sports, Leon Copeman,' she hollered. 'That includes football.'

'I was only kicking their ball back,' I said.

'Well don't. Next time let them get it themselves.'

'OK,' I said, feeling my face redden.

After that I just wandered around. Watching all the other kids having fun made me wish Lenny was with me.

We used to have such a laugh together at lunchtime – playing touch rugby or throwing a tennis ball or playing chase. It didn't matter who else was around when I was with Lenny. Often a crowd of kids would gather around him, chanting for him to perform his famous back flip.

'*Flip, flip, flip.*'

When he'd done it, I used to hold up his hand like he was a boxer who'd just won the world title and everyone would cheer. I was so proud of him.

Suddenly I really missed him. It was almost as though the more kids there were around me, the lonelier I felt. It was like I wasn't a whole person without Lenny. Like everything about me was a bit weaker...like I had a brightness knob and someone had turned it down.

I noticed Arnold sitting against the fence that ran around the edge of the school grounds. He was on his own and looked about as lonely as I felt so I went over and sat next to him.

'What's up?' I said.

Arnold studied the sky. 'What do you mean?'

'I mean how's it going? What do you think of the school?'

Arnold shrugged.

'Where's Callum anyway? I thought he was supposed to be showing you the ropes?'

'What ropes?'

I turned to study Arnold's face. There was no twinkle in his eye, no twitch at the corners of his mouth.

'I just mean Callum was supposed to be looking after you, wasn't he?'

Arnold snorted. 'He left me.'

'No way. What happened?'

'He said he had to get something from his locker. He told me to wait by the water fountain and he'd be back in a minute but he didn't come back.'

'He just abandoned you?'

Arnold nodded. I imagined him waiting forlornly at the drinking fountain, watching kids come and go – eagerly hoping to see Callum return.

'How long were you waiting?'

Arnold frowned at me like I was an idiot. 'A minute,' he replied. 'Just like Callum said.'

'What – exactly a minute?' I said with a slight laugh.

'Exactly,' Arnold confirmed. 'I timed it on my watch.'

'I see,' I paused for a moment then said, 'Do you think maybe it's possible he meant he'd be back in minute or so? Like in a few minutes?'

Arnold shook his head. 'No, he was very specific. He definitely said he'd be back in *a minute*.'

I was about to suggest we go and find Callum and clear up the misunderstanding. But then I caught a glimpse of Callum lurking behind the science block at the far side of the playground. He was laughing at me and making the loser sign with his thumb and forefinger on his forehead. I wasn't sure if he meant Arnold was a loser or I was a loser for sitting with him but either way I realised he had intended to ditch Arnold all along.

'Don't worry about Callum anyway,' I said.

'Why would I be worried?'

'I just meant don't let him get to you. He can be a real idiot sometimes.'

'It's OK. Everybody leaves me sooner or later anyway.'

'What do you mean?' I said.

Arnold shrugged. 'I'm a bit odd. I know that. That's why I have to change schools all the time. It doesn't usually take long for the head teacher to decide I'm a disruptive influence or I don't fit in. Kids are the same – they find me just a bit too awkward to deal with. Everyone gets tired of me and realises things are simpler when I'm not around sooner or later. Usually sooner.'

I turned and looked at Arnold. His face displayed no emotion, as if years of rejection had left him immune to its pain.

'I won't,' I said.

Under his breath – not in a needy way but as if it was an actual fact – Arnold said, 'You will. Everyone does.'

We watched the mass of kids in the playground for a while. Then Arnold said, 'Why did that teacher tell you off?'

'I'm not allowed to play contact sports at school,' I said. 'My mum thinks they're dangerous.'

'Kicking a ball can't be that dangerous?'

'Tell my mum that,' I laughed. 'She'd make me wear a crash helmet to brush my teeth if she had her way.'

'How come?' Arnold asked, raising his voice above the sound of the bell signalling the end of lunch break.

'Because she thinks the bathroom is such a hazardous environment,' I said with mock gravity. 'I might easily have some allergic reaction to the peppermint in the toothpaste. I might faint and, as I collapse, I could easily fall backwards and crack my head on the corner of the bath. You know – the sort of fatal tooth-brushing accident that happens every day. My mum thinks it's such a dangerous activity it's a wonder the government doesn't introduce compulsory safety regulations for it. Like the rules for wearing seatbelts in a car. According to her, brushing your teeth is easily as dangerous as skydiving or lion taming.'

I smiled at Arnold – expecting him to play along with making fun of my mum's overprotective attitude. Or at least to get it. But he just frowned and said, 'I don't think brushing your teeth is dangerous.'

We both got up and started walking towards the school building. I felt awkward that he thought I was being serious about my mum thinking brushing your teeth was an extreme sport. (She is super overprotective, but she's not crazy.) I could have left it at that but I decided to show Arnold I'd been messing about by really going over the top.

'Are you serious?' I said with massively exaggerated surprise. 'You've never stood in your bathroom and thought to yourself, I'm taking my life in my hands just being here? I'll be lucky if I make it out of here alive? It's a wonder they don't make protective clothing mandatory for such a lethal environment?'

Arnold shook his head. Now he was looking at me like I was completely crazy.

'Well, maybe you could come round and explain your opinion to my mum, because she can't run a tap without considering the potential disaster she's flirting with.'

'OK.' Arnold nodded earnestly. 'If you like.'

Feeling relieved that he was finally joining in with my joke I said, 'Why don't you come home with me tonight? In fact, you could stay for the weekend and provide a balanced viewpoint on a whole range of safety issues. My mum won't even listen to me when I tell her that it's safe to climb the stairs without ropes and crampons. But she might listen to you.'

'OK,' he said.

'Great. You could be a sort of guest risk assessor.'

'I could totally do that,' Arnold said, smiling broadly.

'Any time she thinks something is dangerous I'll tell her what I think.'

'Yeah,' I laughed. 'That's a deal.'

Then we went back into the classroom. As I got my books out for double maths I was smiling to myself about the joke Arnold and I had shared.

4

I didn't hang around after school. I didn't want to speak to Ash and Tom because they'd be talking about the rugby match and I didn't want to get involved. It wasn't that I resented their excitement but I missed that feeling just before a match. That nervous anticipation. The team spirit – like one big family. It was easier for me just to stay away and pretend it wasn't happening.

So, when the bell went and Mr Rooney dismissed us, I was first out of my chair.

'In a hurry, Leon?' he said, as I bustled past him, slinging my bag over my shoulder.

'Yes, sir,' I said without breaking stride. Then I was through the door and running down the corridor towards the exit.

The sky was grey. Fat clouds hung low like sagging sheets on a washing line. I tried not to think about the rugby, but I couldn't help it and the more I thought about it the more it felt like my mood was sagging too. I just wished everything could be back to how it used to be. If this semifinal had been a year ago, right now Lenny and I would be in the changing room, looking forward to thrashing the opposition. He'd be going around encouraging each player individually. When he'd get to me he'd just smile and say, 'Do your stuff, Leon,' and I'd reply, 'Same to you, Lenny.' When we used to run out onto the pitch it was like we could take on the whole world together – like nothing could stop us.

But things would never be like that again. Instead of taking on the world with my brother – my best friend – I was dawdling home on my own.

I took a detour through a park. It was pretty deserted but halfway across I got this strange feeling that someone was following me. I knew it was ridiculous but once I'd got the idea in my head I couldn't get rid of it. Eventually, just to prove to myself I was imagining it, I spun round. I knew no one would be there. Which is why I almost jumped out my skin when I saw Arnold, about five yards behind me.

'Are you following me?' I asked, which I realised was a pointless question. If he had been following me there was no way he was going to admit it so his answer was going to be 'No' either way.

'Yes,' Arnold said.

'Oh.'

'You left class pretty quickly.'

I nodded. Arnold and I held each other's stare in what became an uncomfortably long silence. Eventually I cracked. 'So, was there something you wanted?'

Arnold shook his head.

'Why are you following me then?'

'How else am I supposed to find your house?'

'My house?'

'Yeah – the place where you live.'

'I know what my house is,' I said impatiently. 'But why are you bothered about knowing where I live?'

Arnold blinked. 'Because I'm coming to stay for the weekend.'

This really made me laugh. Not only had Arnold remembered our silly conversation at lunchtime, he'd made the effort to follow me halfway home just to continue the joke. I was still laughing when Arnold said, 'What's so funny?'

The look on his face told me he was serious and that's when I stopped laughing.

Arnold continued, 'You invited me to stay. You said you wanted me to *provide a balanced viewpoint on a whole range of safety issues.*'

'I know I said that, Arnold...' I desperately racked

my brain for a suitable excuse. 'And it would be really cool for you to come and stay but unfortunately we haven't asked your mum's permission. She'll want to meet my parents and talk through all the arrangements...'

'I don't see my mum very much,' said Arnold bluntly. 'She's not well enough to look after me.'

'Oh...I'm sorry,' I said. 'What about your dad though? He won't want you to go and stay at a stranger's house just like that, will he?'

'He died when I was nine.'

'Gosh I really am sorry.'

'Don't apologise – I shouldn't think it was your fault,' Arnold replied.

'No, you're right,' I said shaking my head sincerely.

'Why are you wearing that fluorescent tabard?'

I looked down at my day-glow vest, grateful for the change of subject. 'My mum says I have to wear it for safety,' I said. 'So I don't get run over or anything.'

Arnold looked around. The nearest road was about half a kilometre away. 'Not many cars round here,' he said.

I shrugged. 'You can never be too careful.'

'Shall we go then?' asked Arnold. 'I'll tell your mum what I think about the tabard.'

He was so eager I almost wanted to take him home.

But I hadn't so much as had a friend to tea since Lenny's accident. I wasn't sure how my parents would react to having another boy in the house instead of Lenny. I wasn't sure how I'd react.

'So who looks after you then?' I asked quickly.

'I'm with a foster family.'

'That's nice,' I said brightly.

'It's OK.' Arnold nodded. 'My foster parents had to rush off to Scotland on a family emergency – my foster mum's dad, who is really old, had a nasty fall last week.'

'They left you at home all on your own?'

'Well, Barry's looking after me. He's my foster brother. He's seventeen.'

Immediately I saw my chance to put Arnold off the idea of staying at my house. 'But he'd miss you, wouldn't he? And I'm sure he wouldn't be comfortable about you staying the weekend with some kid from school you hardly know – he'd be worried sick.' I gave Arnold a disappointed smile. 'Bummer.'

Arnold's expression didn't change. In fact, I was coming to realise his expression never seemed to change. It was like his face was frozen in this blank mask.

'Barry told his parents he wanted to stay home to study for exams but really he was hoping to have the house to himself so he could have his girlfriend round. My foster parents agreed because they think he's perfect. He was really pleased with himself until they asked him to look after me to save me travelling to Scotland to see an old man in hospital. So Barry's gone to stay with his girlfriend instead. He said I was old enough to look after myself and that he wished he'd had the house to himself when he was thirteen.'

'He just left you?'

'Uh-huh.'

'On your own?'

Arnold nodded. 'Yup.'

I knew that this was the time to be firm. I had to explain that I'd been joking when I'd said he could stay with me for the weekend. He'd probably be a bit embarrassed for getting the wrong end of the stick – maybe a little hurt. But in my heart I knew there was no way my mum would agree to him staying so there was no point in allowing this to go on.

And yet there was something about his blank expression that really got to me. It might have been his small pouting mouth or his big, sad eyes – brown and shiny like an abandoned polar bear. Something about his face gave me the overwhelming urge to help him. Besides, I was feeling lonely myself – thinking about all my friends playing the big rugby match without me. And without

Lenny. And in a strange way I was enjoying Arnold's company – even if he was slightly odd.

So, ignoring the tiny issue of how I was going to break the news to my mum, I said, 'Well, you'd better come home with me then.'

5

'So, do you like rugby?' I asked as Arnold and I ambled home.

'Sure.'

'You look like you'd make a good forward. I bet you could kick a few butts in the front row.'

Arnold stopped and turned to me. 'You're not allowed to kick someone's butt in rugby. That would be a penalty.'

I ignored him. 'My house is just up here,' I said as we turned into my road.

'The houses here are massive,' Arnold said. 'They must be worth a fortune.'

'I guess so.'

'How much is yours worth?'

'I don't know,' I laughed.

'More than a million?'

'Maybe, I'm not sure.'

'More than two?'

'Possibly, I don't really...'

'How much does your dad earn?'

'What do you mean?'

'Money. How much does he get paid per year for doing his job?'

'I don't know. I've never asked.'

'Aren't you interested? Curious?'

'I suppose, but it's none of my business.'

'I'll ask him for you if you like.'

'You're all right. Thanks.'

Mum's car was on our driveway. This was a problem I hadn't expected because I'd assumed she'd be out at her road-safety meeting. I hadn't quite worked out how I was going to break it to her that I'd brought Arnold home – to stay for the weekend.

It would have been a tricky enough conversation if he'd been one of my best friends – someone my mum knew and trusted. Mum always approved of my friends if they had 'nice parents' or came from a 'nice family'. I never understood why grown-ups judged kids by what their parents were like. Roscoe James was the undisputed winner of 'The most unpleasant child in our year' award and his parents were both magistrates. On the other hand, Keira Richardson, whose dad was in prison for stealing a car, was the kindest girl you could ever wish to meet.

Anyway, I needed time to think about how I was going to mention to my mum that I'd brought home a strange boy (meaning both that he was unfamiliar to me and slightly peculiar). Especially as he came from what she would refer to as a 'troubled background'.

'Come and have a look at our summer house,' I said, leading Arnold down the path at the side of the house and into the back garden. 'It's wicked.'

When I didn't hear a reply, I turned round to see Arnold standing by the side door.

I could see Mum in the utility room – just a couple of yards from Arnold. If she opened the door to empty the recycling or something they would be face-to-face. She'd assume he was a burglar and call the police, which would make the whole 'Can my new friend stay for the weekend?' conversation all the trickier.

'Come on,' I said urgently.

'Aren't we going in?' Arnold asked.

'Later,' I said sharply. 'Just come and look at the summer house will you.'

As I marched down the garden I could hear footsteps hurrying behind me.

'Why aren't we going in the house?'

'I said *later*.' I didn't especially like my tone but I was really panicking that my mum was going to see us.

'But it's autumn.' Arnold was next to me now. He was about six inches taller than me and rock solid.

'So what?' I opened the wooden door and we went inside.

'Why are we going to the summer house in autumn?'

'It's just a name. It doesn't literally mean you only use it in the summer. You can use it all year round.' Peering through one of the windows I could see my mum come out of our house.

'Why call it a summer house then?' Arnold wondered. 'Why not call it a garden house or an all-year house?'

I turned to see Arnold sitting on top of a stack of garden chairs, legs swinging like a toddler. 'I don't know why I'm calling it the summer house anyway. That's what Mum always calls it but I normally call it the shed. I do it to annoy her.'

'Why?' Arnold asked.

Mum was striding down the garden towards us. Her arms were folded which meant either she was cross or she was cold.

'Get down!' I barked, ducking from view.

Arnold immediately leaped from his perch and hit the floor, flat on his stomach with his cheek resting on the floorboards.

40

'What is it?' he asked. His voice was flat calm, like it was perfectly normal to dive for cover in someone's garden shed.

'My mum's coming.'

'Why are we hiding?'

I thought for a moment. 'I don't want to scare her. She might get a fright if she sees us here.'

Arnold nodded like this made perfect sense and I felt guilty for lying to him.

'Is she coming this way?' he whispered.

I held my breath and rose onto my haunches to peer into the garden. Mum strode across the lawn to within ten yards of me and I was sure she must have seen us sneaking down the garden. I was still trying to think how I would explain the sturdy boy lying face down on the floor if she came into the summer house when she stopped. Bending next to her herb garden, she picked a few leaves, straightened up and headed back to the house.

'She's going,' I said, exhaling. 'That was a close shave.'

Arnold clambered to his feet and blinked at me. 'Your mum was having a shave?'

I took a couple of garden chairs off the stack and gestured for Arnold to sit in one.

'Are you hungry?' I asked.

Arnold shrugged. 'I suppose so.'

'I could murder some biscuits.'

Arnold looked shocked.

'I mean I'd really enjoy a few biscuits.'

'Me too,' he said eagerly.

'OK. Wait here. I'll be right back.'

6

Mum was studying her laptop at the kitchen table, which was strewn with box files. The spines of the files were labelled with things like 'Harrington Road speed bumps', or 'St Matthew's School zebra crossing'.

'Hi, darling,' she said, peering briefly at me over her glasses. 'Looking forward to the weekend?'

'I suppose,' I said. 'You know...' I wasn't sure what *you know* meant so I'm pretty sure Mum didn't either but she nodded anyway. Maybe she thought asking what *you know* was supposed to mean might lead to a row, or maybe she wasn't really listening.

'I thought you'd be out at your residents' meeting,' I said, picking a couple of apples from the fruit bowl.

'I was just about to leave when I got a message to say the council have agreed to our demand for speed

bumps so there was no need for a strategy meeting.'
Mum did a quiet cheer and made a fist.

'You should be out celebrating,' I said hopefully.

'No time for that.' Mum gestured at the files on the
table. 'Plenty more for me to be getting on with. How was
today anyway?'

'Good.'

'That's good. I mean that *is* good.'

Sometimes talking to Mum was like talking to a
stranger.

'Anything exciting happen?'

'No. Nothing. Just a normal day.'

'You got to school OK? And home again?'

'Obviously. Ha ha.'

Opening various cupboards, I stacked crisps, biscuits
and cans of lemonade onto a tray, whilst trying to shield
it from my mum.

'It's a shame I've got so much on. I've even got meet-
ings on most of this weekend.'

'That's OK.'

'We could have hung out together,' Mum murmured,
almost to herself. 'Had one of our movie nights or something.'

We used to spend a lot of time together, but Mum
and I hadn't done anything with each other since Lenny
was killed. To start with I was way too upset to even think

44

about anything fun. Eventually, after months, that sort of all-consuming hopeless grief lifted. Much later I'd occasionally realise I was having fun and feel guilty. I never wanted to suggest doing something fun in case it seemed disrespectful. It'd been so long now that it was like we'd given up on the idea. We just had this sort of routine where every now and then Mum would say how nice it would be if only we could do something fun. It was like if she said out loud that she was too busy to do stuff together then she'd done all she can. She was the same with exercise. If she wasn't so busy she'd be a champion triathlete or a cross-channel swimmer.

I never suggested doing anything together. If I did, it might put her in the awkward position of turning me down. I'd ask why not and she'd be forced to admit that she didn't want to spend time with me any more. Not after what happened.

'Mum?' I said, sliding my tray out of sight.

'Hmm?'

'Do you think I could have someone over?'

Mum looked up at me. 'Here?' she asked. Her tone was not encouraging.

'Yeah,' I said. 'I always used to have friends over...'

Mum clasped her hands together. 'I don't know, Leon. Who do you have in mind?' Her voice was tight – fearful.

'This weird kid that started at our school today,' was

45

not an answer that would have calmed my mum's nerves. Instead I said, 'One of my school friends.'

'Who?'

'Not sure. He won't be a Kestrels fan though.' I laughed hopefully. Mum didn't. I made a mental note to save the rugby banter for Dad.

'I need to know who.'

'What difference does it make?'

'It makes a huge difference. I need to know that it's someone who is sensible, responsible, trustworthy. I need to be able to communicate with his parents to establish ground rules and boundaries.'

'Why does it have to be such a big deal?' I said, rolling my eyes.

'Listen to me, young man,' she said in an icy whisper. 'Our house is the one place I know you are safe. If you bring other boys into the equation then your behaviour will change. You're more likely to misbehave and take risks and that's when accidents happen.'

'We'd only play on the Xbox or something. It's not like we'd be abseiling off the roof.'

'Well, you never know.'

'I'll take that as a "No" then.'

Mum sighed. 'Take it as a "Tell me who you want to invite and I'll think about it".'

'Great,' I mumbled. 'I must be the only kid in school

who has to submit a risk assessment before having a mate round for tea.'

'That's not what I'm saying.'

'That's what it sounds like,' I said.

Based on the conversation so far I judged it wasn't a good time to tell Mum about Arnold waiting in the summer house for the OK to come and stay in our house for the weekend.

Deciding on another course of action for Arnold, I lifted my tray and tiptoed towards the side door.

With every step I expected Mum to question why I was sneaking into the garden with a tray laden with enough snacks for a fortnight.

'Feeding the five thousand are we?' That's what she used to say when Lenny and I came home from school and grabbed some food to take upstairs to play Xbox.

'Uh – Leon?' she said. Busted. 'Where are you going?'

'Just out. To the summer house. It's nice in there – peaceful.' Mum looked suspicious. To ward off any more questions I sneered, 'Don't worry. I won't burn it down or anything.'

It was like a shadow passed over Mum's face, then she went back to her work. I closed the side door behind me and traipsed down the garden to the summer house.

Arnold and I munched and slurped our way through

the junk-food feast then sat back in our garden chairs holding our bellies.

'That was nice,' he said.

'I am so stuffed,' I said. As I spoke a massive burp rose through my chest and forced its way out of my mouth, blowing my lips apart as it escaped. It made a satisfying belchy sound. Nothing earth shattering but certainly louder than average. About five on the Richter scale.

I glanced at Arnold and gave him a proud nod, expecting him to indicate his approval in a similar way. A burp like that deserved respect.

But Arnold's face didn't display silent admiration. His eyes ballooned and his mouth popped open like a little kid who'd heard the F word for the first time. Then he fell about laughing. Literally fell about. His head went back and he flung himself into his chair, making a noise like an asthmatic donkey. Then he slid forward off his chair and onto his knees before slumping onto the floor clutching his ribs. He rolled about for such a long time that I started to laugh too. Not crazy hysterical laughing like Arnold, just normal. But that seemed to tickle him even more so he went on rolling around for ages.

Eventually he sat up, wheezing and wiping tears from his eyes.

'That was funny,' he groaned.

I liked the fact that my burp seemed to have broken the ice between us. It was the first time we'd both let go since we'd met and it felt good. I wanted to prolong that connection so I said, 'I just wanted to get that off my chest.' I started laughing and it was a good few seconds before I realised this time I was on my own. Arnold's face showed no sign of amusement. Nothing.

'What?' he said.

'Sorry?' I wheezed.

'What did you want to get off your chest?'

'I mean, I'm glad I brought it up,' I giggled.

'Brought what up?' he frowned.

'It's a joke,' I said, beginning to wish I hadn't bothered. 'When you bring something up you mention it in conversation.'

'So?'

'But you can also bring up a burp. From your guts.' I swept my hand upwards from my stomach to illustrate what I was saying. 'It's a double meaning.'

'So what's the joke?'

I fumbled for the words to explain what was a pretty feeble pun in the first place. In the end I retorted with, 'Well, what's so funny about a burp?'

Arnold's mouth spread into the broadest grin. 'Burps are just funny. Everyone knows that.'

7

Arnold and I were sitting in the dark, huddled up with our knees under our chins. The sugar-rush I'd got from the snacks had long since passed, leaving me feeling tired and empty. I was beginning to suspect Arnold's initial excitement at the idea of hanging out in the summer house was beginning to wear a little thin. Neither of us had spoken for about half an hour.

'When can we go in?' Arnold's voice sounded strangely loud in the dark.

'Soon.'

'Won't your mum wonder where you are?'

That was a good point. Soon Mum would start looking for me. If we hid, she'd panic and think I'd been kidnapped, or something. If she found me in the summer house with Arnold she'd think he was holding me hostage. Both scenarios would finish with her freaking out and calling the police.

I glanced at my watch. Six-thirty. Kneeling by the wood-panelled wall I peered through the window. Across the black lawn a couple of rectangles glowed orange on the dark silhouette of my house. The kitchen and Olivia's room. Olivia was probably sketching outfits on her art pad, listening to impossibly cool music on her iPod. I imagined Mum standing at the hob cooking something tasty and listening to classical music that was supposed to depict a battle or a storm or something. I could almost feel the heat from the central heating. A sudden shiver rippled through my body.

I realised I really hadn't thought this through properly. An evening of adventure camped out in the summer house had seemed like a pretty fun plan – just to tide us over until tomorrow when I'd hoped to come up with a better arrangement. But the temperature was already dropping towards freezing. There was no way Arnold could sleep out here, no matter how many duvets I managed to smuggle out of the house.

'Here's the plan,' I said, turning to Arnold. His eyes seemed to twinkle as he listened eagerly to my idea.

I turned the handle and opened the door, telling myself to act natural.

'Only me!' I announced. So far so good. Or maybe

announcing it was 'only me' was exactly what someone would say if they had something, or someone, to hide. 'I mean, obviously it's only me. Who else would I have with me? I mean if I'd met Owen Ritchie on the way home I might have invited him for tea, but that's highly unlikely so who else would I bring home? Certainly not a peculiar foster-kid who's just started at our school and who I hardly know.'

I clapped a hand over my mouth. My last sentence seemed to reverberate around the huge kitchen just beyond the open utility room doorway. I considered cowering in the corner until everyone in the kitchen had forgotten what I'd just said. Except that my role was to provide a distraction for Arnold who was about to let himself in through the front door. Maybe I was taking too long. Maybe Arnold had already let himself in.

I burst into the kitchen, half expecting to see Mum facing Arnold off in the hallway but she was stooped over a counter dicing cucumber.

'Hey, Mum, how you doin'?' I said.

'Hello,' she said. 'I didn't hear you come in.'

Really? 'That's cool, man.'

'Why are you talking all American? You sound like a sales assistant from Hollister.'

'That's real funny. You're a blast.'

Mum peered at me over her glasses. I tried to think

of something else to say – to continue the guise of normality I had already created so successfully. Before I could speak though I heard the unmistakeable sound of a key sliding into the front door. Mum heard it too. I knew she heard it because there was a subtle change in her expression. And because she said, 'Someone's at the door.'

As she turned to head for the hall I knew I had to think fast. I had to say something clever to distract her. But there's a big difference between knowing you have to say something clever and actually saying it. I discovered this when, unable to think what to say I watched help-lessly as she walked towards the hallway.

'OWWWW!' I screamed.

Mum spun round to see what had happened. I was just standing there so Mum looked really confused. As a bit of an afterthought I threw myself onto the floor and writhed around, clutching my knee up to my chest.

OK, it wasn't clever but it worked.

Mum scurried over to me. Kneeling beside me she asked what the matter was. I kept writhing around in the style of a professional footballer trying to get an opponent sent off.

'Leon,' Mum said. 'What's the matter?'

'I think it's cramp,' I said, clenching my teeth and squeezing my eyes tightly shut. 'In my calf.'

'Just lie back,' Mum said, pulling my leg straight and pushing my toes towards my kneecap. 'How's that?'

'Bit better,' I said, nodding bravely. 'I think it's passing.'

'You gave me a fright.' Mum combed her fingers through my hair. 'I thought something terrible had happened.'

'It just came on all of a sudden,' I said, limping towards a dining chair.

As my mum ran me a glass of water from the tap, I tried to peer into the hall. I couldn't see anyone but I felt a gust of cold air on my face. Mum must have felt it too because she placed the glass on the table next to me and marched into the hallway.

I had to cause another diversion but, short of a second bout of cramp, my mind was blank. Mum stopped in the middle of the hall, facing the front door, and planted her hands on her hips.

'What in God's name do you think you're doing?' she demanded.

I followed her into the hallway, remembering to limp just in case she turned back. Expecting to see Arnold trapped like a rabbit in headlights I got ready to look shocked by the stranger's intrusion.

The front door was wide open – the warm house sucking in a constant gale of frigid night air. In the corner of the hall, half standing, half leaning, was a figure. Mum and I exchanged a glance. I felt a mixture of amusement and confusion.

I was confused because the figure in the hallway was my dad, not Arnold. He'd obviously had a few drinks. I was amused because I hadn't seen him tipsy for ages.

'Hey, whizz kid,' he chuckled.

'Looks like your dad's been out celebrating something,' Mum commented.

'A very productive meeting with Mr Schultz as it happens,' Dad announced proudly. Tossing his jacket over the banister he did a little skip and clicked his heels together mid-air.

I smiled and looked at Mum who just shook her head.

Dad ruffled my hair as he passed me on his way to the living room. I went to the front door (remembering to limp about halfway there), stuck my head outside and peered around.

'Arnold?' I whispered urgently. I waited and repeated his name. Nothing.

'I'm just going to check something,' I said to Mum and stepped outside. I stalked about in the front garden for a bit calling Arnold like he was a lost cat. When he didn't show I hurried down the garden and into the summer house, expecting to find him curled up on the floor. But it was empty.

I returned to the front garden and went back into the

hall, closing the door behind me. Mum was just coming out of the living room.

She raised a quizzical eyebrow at me.

'I had this weird feeling I'd left my bike in the garden, but I hadn't.'

Mum nodded slowly – almost suspiciously.

'Everything else all right?' Mum asked.

I shrugged. 'Yeah. Sure.'

But everything wasn't all right at all. Everything was the opposite of all right. Arnold was missing.

8

I did a lap of the kitchen – all natural so Mum wouldn't suspect anything.

'Still looking for your bike?' she asked, stirring something in a saucepan.

'Bike?' I said, without thinking.

'Yes – the bike you thought you'd left outside.'

'Oh right. Yeah. I mean no. I'm just, you know, walking. About. Walking about.' Like I said, all natural. What I was actually doing was checking that Arnold hadn't sneaked in and hidden behind the bin or under the table. He hadn't.

'Casserole smells nice,' I said as I left the room.

'It's not casserole,' Mum called after me. 'It's a *cassoulet*.'

I strolled casually into the living room where Dad was watching the news.

'Hi, Dad,' I said, peering behind the sofa.

My dad turned his head and smiled at me. His mood seemed to have changed since he'd come through the door. He was serious now. Sombre, even. Maybe that was the effect this house had on him. Too many memories.

'Hey, Leon,' he said, clapping his hands together like they were cymbals. 'How was school today?'

'Fine I guess.'

'Good.'

Dad looked back at the TV. I waited for a moment but he seemed engrossed in the news so I turned to leave.

'I miss him, you know,' Dad said, his eyes watery. I couldn't remember the last time he'd referred to Lenny in any way. I guessed the alcohol allowed him to say stuff he'd normally bottle up.

'Me too,' I said.

There was a long, awkward pause then Dad said, 'It wasn't your fault.'

I never said it was, I thought. 'Thanks,' I said.

He said, 'Listen, Leon – you couldn't have done anything else.'

But what I heard was – *if only you'd done things differently*.

'Sure.' I nodded. 'Maybe we should talk about this in the morning?' But I knew we wouldn't. In the morning

58

Dad would be sober and neither of us would want to bring this up. Nobody wanted to bring a downer on the day by talking about Lenny's death over breakfast.

As I turned to leave Dad said, 'I don't get it, Leon. One minute he was here, the next he was gone.'

'I know, Dad.'

'Where did he go?'

I turned back wearily and said, 'He's gone, Dad. He's in heaven now.' I didn't know if I really believed in heaven but I'd have liked to. It'd be cool if Lenny had been up there doing back flips and running riot amongst the angels – stealing their halos and playing their harps.

Dad looked confused. 'I wasn't talking about Lenny.'

'Who were you talking about then?'

'The kid.'

I froze. 'What kid?'

'The kid at the door. He said he was here to see you.'

'Where is he now?'

'I told him to wait on the doorstep.' Dad turned to face the TV. 'As I opened the door, I dropped my keys. I bent down to pick them up and when I turned round, he'd disappeared.' If Arnold wasn't in the kitchen, lounge or hall there was only one other route he could have taken. I legged it up the stairs and bumped into Olivia as she came out her bedroom.

'Oh you're out at last,' she said.

59

'Out?'

'I've been waiting to get in the bathroom for ages. Thought you'd fallen down the loo, or something.'

I laughed with my sister, peering past her along the landing. I always closed my bedroom door. Always. But now it was ajar.

'I'm going out in an hour and I haven't even washed my hair yet.'

'OMG. Hashtag emergency!' I sidled past her and backed towards my room. 'Go, go, go.'

'Is everything all right?'

'Dandy,' I said doing a weird two-thumbs-up thing.

'Dandy?' Olivia laughed, watching me edge away from her.

'Hot date?' I asked.

Olivia shook her head. 'Just a coffee with Beth.'

'Well, have fun. Say hi to good old Bethy, A.K.A. the Bethster.'

Olivia half-smiled, mimicked the two-thumbs-up thing I was still doing and went into the bathroom.

I pushed open my bedroom door and went in, closing it fast behind me. Arnold was lying on my bed, holding a framed photograph, which lived on my bedside table.

'I met your dad,' he said. 'He seemed pretty happy.'

'Yup.'

'Is he celebrating something?'

'I think he's had a good day at work.'

Arnold nodded at the picture in his hands. 'You didn't say you're a twin.'

'I'm not.'

I stepped forward and took the photo from him, replaced it exactly where it had come from. It was a snap taken almost exactly a year ago at the rugby match between the Panthers and the Kestrels. The two teams were bitter rivals so the home game against the Kestrels was always the biggest match of the season. We'd all gone to cheer on the Panthers. Mum, Dad, me, Lenny – even Olivia had come along. She said she was only there to check out who was the best-looking player but I think she really enjoyed it.

Mum had asked a passer-by to take the photo. She'd wanted a 'nice, normal' photo of all of us. One she could send to relatives and show to friends. The more she'd begged us to pose nicely, the more Lenny had fooled around. In the picture, we were all smiling normally except Lenny who was gurning crazily – hooked fingers stretching his mouth and eyes crossed. One fat tear of pure joy was rolling down his rosy cheek.

We all looked so happy – decked out in black and gold scarves – arms round each other like a solid scrum. A unit. A family. It turned out to be the last thing we all did together.

Lenny was killed the following day.

'You look like twins,' Arnold said.

'Uh-huh.'

'But you just said you haven't got a twin?'

'I *had* a twin,' I said. 'I haven't any more.'

Arnold sat up straight and swung his feet onto the floor. One green toe peeked through the hole in his trainer like a turtle's head.

'What happened? Did he die?'

'No, he was beamed up by aliens,' I said.

Arnold looked at me blankly. 'I don't understand.'

'Of course he died.'

'So why did you say he'd been beamed up by aliens?'

'Sorry. I just thought it was obvious that he must have died when I said I haven't got a twin any more.'

'Oh.'

I dropped into the chair at my desk. Swivelled around a bit.

'Do you take everything people say literally?' I asked.

'What do you mean?'

I thought for a moment. 'What would you think if I said someone had egg on their face?'

'What, like runny egg? Dribbling down their chin?' He smiled.

'No.' I laughed. 'It's an expression. It just means they're embarrassed.'

'Why not just say that then? It'd be quicker than saying about the egg. And clearer.'

'True. I guess you don't get sarcasm, either?'

He shook his head. 'I know it's when people say something they don't mean. Or the opposite of what they mean. I just don't get how you're supposed to know which it is though.'

'By how someone says it. If I said to you "nice jumper" it would mean "I like your jumper".'

'OK.'

'But if I said, "*nice jumper*",' I said, with heavy sarcasm, 'it would mean "man, that's a really dodgy jumper". See the difference?'

Arnold looked at me for a moment, nodding thoughtfully.

'No,' he said at last. 'They both sounded like a compliment to me.'

'You're a bit of a fruitcake, d'you know that?'

After a brief pause Arnold clicked his fingers, smiling. 'That's an expression right?'

'Right. I just mean you're pretty unique.'

'And when you said your brother was beamed up by aliens, you were being sarcastic?'

'Bingo!' I reached over and high-fived Arnold.

We both laughed for a bit then he said, 'That's sad about your brother.'

I shrugged like I always do when people say that. Then I waited because people normally don't know what to say next so there's a sort of respectful silence before they change the subject. It's natural I suppose. No one wants to talk about death and everyone's terrified of putting their foot in it – saying the wrong thing or upsetting me.

'Was he murdered?'

'Sorry?'

'Was he murdered? You know – killed by someone?'

'Yeah – I know what murdered means, Arnold. And no, he wasn't.'

'Cancer?'

I shook my head. 'It was an accident. He ran across a road without looking. Someone was driving faster than they should have been and knocked him down.'

'Was there any blood?'

'What kind of question is that?'

'I've often wondered what actually kills someone in that situation...'

'You can't ask stuff like that.'

'Why not?'

Arnold's innocent expression softened my resolve. 'He had massive head injuries, OK? He died instantly.'

'That's good.'

'*Good*?'

'I mean it's good that it was quick. Imagine if he'd been trapped under the car, conscious but in agony, writhing around and dying a slow painful death.'

'Thanks for that, Arnold.'

'I'm just saying he was lucky.'

'Lucky? Lottery winners are lucky. Lenny was run over and killed on his way to school. It's hardly the jackpot is it?'

'I just meant...' Arnold sighed. Chewed his lip. 'Were you there?'

I nodded.

'What was it like?'

'Are you always this direct?'

'If you don't want to talk about it...'

I sort of snorted at this but realised that I actually did want to talk about it. I hadn't ever talked about it because people were usually too tactful to ask. People at school avoided me because they were scared of saying something insensitive. Even my friends didn't talk to me so much because they didn't know what to say. I just spent my life wrapped in lonely, polite silence. Arnold's direct curiosity was a welcome change.

'It was surreal,' I said. 'Mum was with us. Lenny and I were charging about, playing chase. One minute he was laughing and running and full of life. A second later – a split second – he was gone. All the joy and mischief and life had been knocked out of him. I remember the car screeching and Mum screaming. I remember clinging onto her. That was the best I could do. If only I'd warned him somehow – or tried to grab him…'

I picked up the photo from my bedside table and stared at Lenny for a while.

'When we used to go out in the car all together, the whole family, I used to have this recurring disaster fantasy. I'd imagine our car veering off the road and ending up sinking in a watery ditch. Everyone would be unconscious except me. I'd undo my seatbelt and somehow manage to break a window and swim free dragging my sister with me. When I'd pulled her to safety I'd go back into the water. Holding my breath, I'd dive down again and again, rescuing my mum and dad. Finally, I'd save Lenny.'

'Why was he last?'

'I don't know. It was like a Hollywood movie. Saving him was the big finish – what everything else had been building up to. In my fantasy, I was some kind of hero. Stupid, isn't it? When my chance came to be an actual hero I chickened out.'

'What happened?'

'I remember seeing the car. Lenny didn't see it but I did. I remember him stepping into the road. I knew he was going to get hit and I did nothing. Instead I clung onto my mum like a baby.'

'Do you blame yourself?'

I shrugged. 'I sometimes think, "If only things had happened differently that morning." Like, if we hadn't been playing chase in the first place he probably wouldn't have run into the road. But we couldn't have known what was about to happen, I suppose. Mostly I can persuade myself that a game of chase is a pretty normal thing for kids to do.

'The thing that really haunts me is that I saw the car coming before Lenny did. In that split second I should have shouted or pushed him out of the car's way or...something. I should have done *something*.'

'What about your parents?'

'What about them?'

'Do they blame you?'

'They don't actually say it's my fault, but sometimes I feel like that's what they're thinking.'

'How?'

'I just can OK?'

'I don't see how you can tell someone blames you if they haven't said they blame you.'

'No. Well you wouldn't, would you? You can't even tell when someone's being sarcastic.'

'That's true,' Arnold said quietly, turning his head away from me slightly. I swivelled in my chair, feeling mean and wishing I hadn't snapped. I wondered if he was trying not to cry but then he jumped off the bed and loped across the room. Grabbing an Xbox controller, he turned and beamed at me. 'Wanna play FIFA?'

'Sure. But don't cry when I whoop your butt.' Catching Arnold's eye I added, 'Don't worry. That's just an expression.'

9

Arnold turned out to be a really good loser. He lost about ten matches in a row but his eager, puppy-like enthusiasm never wavered.

Mum called me down for tea but I said I wasn't hungry. When I went downstairs a while later the light was on in Mum's study and Dad was snoring in his armchair. My dinner was keeping warm in the oven so I put it on a tray, along with some drinks and fruit and chocolate and headed back upstairs.

Arnold and I huddled round the plate.

'The casserole's awesome.' Arnold was bent over, scooping chunks of sausage and chicken into his mouth.

'It's a *cassoulet*,' I said without thinking.

'What's a *cassoulet*?'

'I don't know.' I shrugged – worried that I might seem weird for correcting him. 'What this is, I suppose. That's

69

what Mum called it. I think it's French. She loves anything French.' I said this like it was really lame but Arnold just smiled.

'My mum loves French food, too.' He looked into thin air, a blob of sauce on his chin. 'She calls it *cuisine*.'

It was the perfect opportunity to ask more about his parents but something stopped me. Probably the same thing that stops most people asking me about Lenny. I didn't want to pry. I didn't want to make him feel awkward. I didn't want to make *myself* feel awkward.

'Doesn't she mind?' Arnold said, and the moment to ask about his mother had passed.

'Mind what?'

'You bringing your food up here?'

I shook my head. 'She's not bothered so long as I'm *safe and sound*. We never eat together any more anyway. Mum cooks but hardly ever sits with us – she always finds other stuff to do. Washing, ironing, emailing, anything to avoid all of us doing something together. If Dad's at work she might sit down, but then if he comes home when we're eating he won't join us. It's like they're terrified of having us all round the table because then there would be just one empty chair.'

'Lenny's.'

'It's like if we all do our own thing – keep moving – we can forget that we're a man down. They're terrified that if we all have dinner or watch TV or whatever they'd be unable to cope with the gap Lenny's left. So they make sure we don't do anything together. Ever.'

Arnold shook his head. 'That's pretty sad.'

When we'd eaten we played on the Xbox again. About half-ten I heard footsteps climbing the stairs. Instinctively I knew it was my mum – and that she was going to come into my room.

'You have to hide,' I whispered.

'Why?' Arnold said. 'Where?'

Desperately scanning my room, I wondered where I could hide Arnold if Mum came in. Under the bed? Would be a good idea if it wasn't crammed full of old junk. Ditto my wardrobe. Behind the door? Yup, that was the best I could come up with.

'I'll explain after,' I said, grabbing Arnold's arm and pulling him towards the door. 'Stand here and don't move.'

As the door opened, Arnold pressed his back against the wall. The door stopped about an inch from his nose. My mum stood in the doorway, one hand resting on the handle.

'I'm going to bed now,' she said.

'OK. Goodnight.' I had just sat back on my bed, pretending to be engrossed in my video game.

'I've got lots of appointments this weekend so I'll be out of the house about eight. Back around five I expect.'

'OK.' I glanced up and smiled, trying not to react to the sight of Arnold, pinned between the door and the wall – just inches from my mum. 'Is Dad going to be around?'

Mum gave me a sad smile. 'I expect he'll be going into the office. He's crazy busy right now.'

I nodded.

'Don't forget your appointment with Dr Laughlin tomorrow. Ten a.m. You'll need to leave by nine to get there in plenty of time – you don't want to be rushing.'

'I know,' I said, tetchily.

'What else have you got planned for tomorrow?'

I shrugged. 'Oh, just some base jumping and a spot of wing walking.'

'Don't be smart with me, Leon.'

'Sorry. I'm just going to hang out. Nothing special.'

'Fine – just so long as you're sensible. Well, keep in touch. Goodnight.'

'Night, Mum.'

As Mum closed the door behind her, Arnold and I both let out a long breath.

'Why was I hiding?' Arnold asked. 'Why not just introduce me?'

'It's just a bit late,' I said, feigning a yawn. 'Mum's so hospitable she'd have insisted we go downstairs and have milk and cookies and I'd quite like to play a bit more Xbox, that's all.'

'But you definitely asked her if it was OK for me to stay?'

I crossed my fingers behind my back and said, 'Absolutely.'

'Who's Dr Laughlin?'

'My bereavement counsellor,' I muttered – the very fact that I had a counsellor was a depressing reminder of the state my life was in. 'I see her every week to help me cope with Lenny's death.'

'Does it – help?'

'I don't know.' I thought for a moment. 'Some of the stuff we do is really tough. Last week I wrote a letter to Lenny.'

'What did you write?'

'I just told him the rugby scores and about school and stuff. I joked that Olivia's hair still looks like she's been in an explosion in a hairspray factory. I said Mum and Dad were OK but they've changed – everything has changed. I said they miss him. I said I was sorry I didn't save him. I asked him to forgive me for not warning him about the car or dragging him out of its way. I told him I was sorry for being such a scaredy-cat when he needed me most. And I said that I miss him. That I really, really miss him.'

A sort of uncontrollable sadness came over me and

73

I put my face in my hands, sobbing silently – my whole body shaking.

'What did you do with the letter?' Arnold asked.

I sniffed hard and wiped a sleeve across my nose, making a slimy streak on my sweatshirt. 'We tied it to a helium balloon and let it go. It was like sending it up to heaven.' I managed to blurt the words out before more sadness doubled me over.

After a short pause Arnold said, 'But it won't really get to heaven.'

'Sorry?'

'The letter won't actually get to heaven.' Something about Arnold's perplexed expression amused me.

Wiping my face I smiled. 'I know.'

'So what's the point of sending it then?' Arnold's confusion had turned into indignation. 'Why send a letter you know will never be delivered. It doesn't make sense.'

'You're funny, Arnold,' I said, laughing.

'Why?'

'You just are. Thank you.'

'What for?'

Olivia came home about midnight. I knew if she saw my light on she'd come in and say hi so I opened my door as she got to the top of the stairs.

'Hey, big sis,' I said, squeezing my body into the narrow gap I'd created in the doorway.

'Hey, *lil bro*,' she replied with a quizzical frown.

'What's up?'

'Not much. You?'

'The usual.' I sighed. 'You know, hanging out. On my own. Just me. Alone.'

She leaned towards me and sniffed. 'Have you been drinking?'

'No diggedy, sistah,' I replied, wondering why I'd started talking like a rapper.

'Okey dokey.' Olivia's eyes narrowed. 'Sleep tight, Kanye.'

Arnold and I played games until about two a.m. I didn't hear Dad come upstairs. Maybe he went to bed later, maybe he slept in his armchair all night.

The next morning I woke to find Arnold's green-socked feet staring me in the face. I pushed them away and sat up. The clock on my bedside table said it was nearly half-ten. The house was quiet.

I was desperate for the loo so I tried to clamber over Arnold without waking him. Unfortunately I got the duvet caught under my elbow so I fell on top of him, kneeing him in the thigh.

'Dead leg!' he shouted, half laughing and half crying.

'Sorry,' I laughed, peering through my curtains at the empty driveway.

Arnold rolled out of bed and started hopping around the room. 'Man that hurts,' he groaned.

'Come on, tough guy,' I said, once I'd been to the loo. 'The best thing for a dead leg is to walk it off.'

'Walk? Where to?'

'The kitchen,' I grinned. 'I'm starving.'

I motioned for Arnold to wait on the landing as I crept downstairs. Empty bowls and coffee cups in the kitchen sink told me the coast was clear. From the hallway I beckoned Arnold down and he followed me into the kitchen.

'Where is everyone?' Arnold asked.

'Dad'll be in the office working on his latest deal. Mum's probably out recording the number of cars speeding down some residential street,' I said. As I spoke I noticed a note clamped to the fridge by a magnet. 'Speak of the devil,' I said, snatching it off.

It was from my mum, telling me to eat some fruit and not to run across roads or talk to strangers or climb trees or stick metal cutlery into the toaster or poke my fingers into electrical sockets...I stopped reading at the bottom of the page, and sighed. Instead of turning the sheet over to read the rest of my mum's cautionary advice I screwed up the note and tossed it into the bin.

'Sorry to spoil your fun today, Arnold,' I said. 'But my mum says we mustn't lie on train tracks and wait for the intercity to run us over. And jumping down abandoned wells is out too, I'm afraid.'

'Why would we do that?' Arnold asked.

'Exactly. Why would we?' I said, shaking my head. 'What do you fancy for breakfast?'

Arnold slid onto a stool at the breakfast bar. 'What have you got?'

I pulled open the fridge door and gazed inside. 'Everything,' I said.

After a breakfast of cereal, toast, smoothie, scrambled eggs and (really, really) crispy bacon, Arnold sat back in his chair.

'I've never had black bacon before,' he said. 'Is it a French thing?'

'Sure,' I said. 'Don't tell me you've never eaten bacon *noir*?'

'I don't think so.' He popped the last piece of burnt meat into his mouth and gazed round the room. 'This is a huge house. Your parents must be pretty successful?'

'Depends what you call successful.'

'I mean moneywise. Your dad must be *really* wealthy.'

'If you start asking me how much he earns again I might have to kill you.'

'That's an expression ... right?'

'No, I'm serious. Deadly serious.'

Arnold looked horrified and I started laughing. 'I'm going to have to give you some sort of signal to let you know when I'm joking. How about this...'

I clapped then spread my arms wide, shimmying my open hands.

'What sort of signal is that supposed to be?' he asked.

'Jazz hands,' I said. 'If you see me doing it, you'll know not to take me seriously. OK?'

Arnold didn't look too certain but he nodded.

'Cool. Now can you do the washing-up and tidy my room while I watch some TV?'

Arnold looked pretty annoyed, then I did the jazz hands thing and he grinned.

'That actually works,' he said. 'I like it.'

'So what do you really want to do today?'

Arnold looked around thoughtfully. He fixed his gaze on the French windows that stretched across the back of our kitchen. Beyond our patio the morning dew twinkled on the vast expanse of flat manicured lawn.

'How about some football in the garden?' he said.

'Or we could play some FIFA? I'll go easy on you this time.'

'I'd rather play football.'

'The thing is,' I said, pulling a face, 'I'm not allowed to play football in the garden – Mum thinks it's too dangerous.'

'What about cricket?'

'She knows I don't play cricket,' I laughed. 'Never have.'

I saw a glint in Arnold's eye. 'Let's play cricket then.'

'I'd say cricket is a lot more dangerous than football, wouldn't you?' I said. 'Especially in a confined space like my garden.'

Arnold looked suddenly concerned. 'Has your mum told you not to play it then?'

'No, but only because I never play it,' I laughed. 'She hasn't expressly forbidden me from shooting the windows with an air rifle, either.'

The concern on Arnold's face had changed to confusion. 'Would you rather shoot an air rifle then?'

'No,' I said as calmly as I could. 'I was just explaining why my mum has never forbidden me from playing cricket in the garden.'

'Great,' Arnold was beaming now. 'Cricket it is then. I saw some gear in the summer house last night.'

'Oh right. Yeah – that was Lenny's. He loved his cricket.'

'It'll be a laugh,' said Arnold. 'Come on.'

Fifteen minutes later we'd showered and dressed and I was following Arnold down the garden towards the summer house.

'I really don't know about this,' I said as Arnold opened

79

the summer-house door and went in. He reappeared a moment later holding a netting bag that contained Lenny's cricket gear.

'What don't you know?' Arnold opened the bag and tipped out the stumps and bails and the bat.

'Whether this is a good idea.'

By now Arnold had skewered the lawn with a single stump and was heading away from me, pacing out the wicket.

'Is it twenty or twenty-two yards?' he called.

'I don't know. Twenty-two, I think. Look, I really don't think we should...'

Arnold said nothing as he knocked three stumps into the ground using the handle of the bat. I winced with each blow, imagining my dad's reaction if he ever discovered the three evenly spaced holes drilled into his perfect lawn. When Arnold had balanced the bails on the stumps he stepped back to admire his handiwork.

'Do you want to bat or bowl?'

I knew that playing cricket in the garden was a bad idea. Mum would have had a fit if she knew what I was doing – and yet there was no arguing with Arnold's logic. I had never been told that I mustn't play cricket in the garden. She had reminded me over and over not to do countless other things that were clearly more stupid and dangerous than playing cricket – like sticking my fingers

80

into electrical sockets, for instance. So I managed to kid myself that maybe, just maybe, she hadn't forbidden cricket in the garden because it was one of the few sports she deemed to be acceptable.

But there was something else. Arnold reminded me of Lenny begging me to play cricket with him. Last summer we'd been on holiday to Cornwall for a fortnight. There was a massive field near our cottage and every day Lenny used to plead with me to go over with him and play cricket. I'd always refused. I'd said it was because I didn't like cricket but it was really because I wasn't any good at it.

Looking back, I thought how much fun it would have been. We'd have laughed so much together at my wayward bowling or me slashing the bat at thin air. But at the time I couldn't bear the prospect of embarrassing myself. If it had been the other way round I knew Lenny would have agreed like a shot. I will always regret disappointing him like that – always wish I could have the chance again to bowl a few balls at my brother.

I smiled at Arnold and said, 'I'll bowl.'

I reversed about ten paces from the single stump, pretending to polish the ball on my trousers. I started my run-up, accelerating from a trot to canter, did a little skip and bowled the ball overarm. It all felt pretty profes-sional to me but I must have released the ball way too

81

early because it sailed high towards Arnold's head without bouncing. He ducked out of the way and the ball skipped off the patio and struck the middle of one of the French doors with a sickening thud.

The reflection of the garden in the glass sort of stretched then pinged back to normal as the window bowed with the impact. The ball bounced back, rolled across the patio and trickled to a stop on the lawn.

Arnold turned to face me, his eyes wide.

I was about to give him the 'I told you this was a bad idea' speech but then he burst out laughing. Again, this wasn't your normal teenage snigger but the now-familiar full-on Arnold hysteria. Letting the bat fall, he dropped to his knees and rolled onto the grass doing the asthmatic donkey thing.

'It's not funny,' I said. Arnold continued rolling around, tears of joy making his eyes shiny.

'Come on,' he gasped. 'How can you say that's not funny?'

'What if it had smashed?'

'It would never break,' Arnold said, getting to his feet. 'The glass is too strong.'

'Oh and you're some sort of glass expert, are you?' I sneered, all, you know...sneery.

'My foster dad works in double glazing, so...' Arnold picked up the ball and tossed it to me, smiling.

'Oh,' I said, catching the ball.

'The windows are made of toughened safety glass. You could hit them with a sledgehammer and they wouldn't break.'

'So we couldn't break them even if we tried?' I felt suddenly relieved. 'And you knew that all along?'

Arnold smiled his big smile. 'The only windows that aren't toughened glass are the upstairs ones.' He turned and pointed to the bedroom windows. 'And you'd have to be really rubbish to slice the ball that high.'

I delivered my next ball with less speed and more accuracy than my first. Arnold stroked it away with a straight bat, sending the ball trundling into the flowerbed beyond the summer house. He started his run and I scampered away to field the ball. Four balls later Arnold scooped the ball high in the air for an easy catch.

'OK, seven runs to beat,' I said as I took the bat from Arnold. I was feeling pretty confident. Seven wasn't exactly a massive target.

As Arnold started his run up I beat the tip of my bat on the grass, grinding the handle in my palms. His delivery was slow and looping. I waited for it to bounce. It skipped off the moist grass, coming up towards my waist. I stepped back and swiped my bat in a flat circle. The ball was almost behind me when I made contact. As the bat continued its swing I watched the ball fly off its top edge and spin high into the air and backwards towards the house.

There was surprisingly little noise as the ball punched through Olivia's bedroom window. Just a crisp crunching sound that only lasted a split second. It wasn't even very loud.

I allowed myself a moment to assess the situation. Whichever way you looked at it there was a definite jagged hole in the glass of Olivia's bedroom window. Fact.

The thoughts that went through my head in that moment, in no particular order, were these.

Mum is going to kill me.

Dad is going to kill me.

Olivia . . . she's probably going to kill me, too.

Basically I was dead. So it came as little comfort when I looked round to see Arnold rolling around on the floor again. At last he managed to catch his breath and the asthmatic donkey noise began to bellow from his mouth.

Brilliant. I was going to be strung up for breaking the rules (and my sister's bedroom window) and all Arnold could do was laugh. I was feeling angry, and indignant and scared all at the same time. Which made it all the more weird that I started laughing, too.

I didn't go as far as rolling around on the floor like Arnold (I wasn't four years old for heaven's sake) but I was in total fits for some time. It actually felt pretty good.

I hadn't laughed so hard for ages – not since Lenny was alive.

Eventually Arnold wiped a hand across his eyes. 'See. I told you a quick game of cricket would be fun.'

'You were right. I had a *smashing* time.'

I smiled but by now Arnold had stopped laughing.

10

We decided my best defence was to plead ignorance. If I denied all knowledge, then how could anyone prove that I'd smashed the window? However suspicious Mum and Dad might be, there would still be an element of doubt. Maybe a bird had lost its bearings and flown through the window, I would argue. Dazed and confused it might have lain on Olivia's bed for a while to gather its senses before flying back into the wild through the hole in the glass.

It could happen.

That plan was scuppered though when we discovered Olivia's bedroom door was locked. It would have been tricky to explain the presence of the cricket ball in the bedroom as well as putting the blame on a wayward bird. I rang Olivia's mobile but there was no answer so I sent her a text. I put, 'Hi. Please don't tell M & D about the cricket ball in your bedroom. Say it must have been a bird.'

I realised after I'd sent it that it probably wouldn't make much sense to my sister but that didn't really matter. When she got the message, she'd call to ask what I was talking about and I could explain. Olivia took her phone with her everywhere so I expected her to call pretty soon. In the meantime Arnold and I made some squash and watched TV.

A report came on about this season's meeting of the Panthers and the Kestrels. The Panthers were hoping to repeat their resounding victory from last season. It seemed like only yesterday we'd watched the same game last season. They played some highlights from that match and it brought it all back to me. Me and Lenny cheering like crazy. Mum and Dad beaming, almost giddy with happiness. Olivia trying hard all day not to let on she was having the time of her life.

'That's the match we went to last year,' I said. 'Where the picture by my bed was taken.'

'When is this year's match?'

'Tomorrow.'

'We should go.'

'Sure,' I laughed. 'The match has probably been sold out for weeks.'

'Someone's bound to be selling tickets.'

'We might be able to pick up a couple I suppose.'

'I meant everyone. Just like last year. Your whole family – except for Lenny.'

'Obviously.' I thought about Arnold's suggestion for a moment. 'I don't know, Arnold. My family haven't even sat around a table together since Lenny was killed. I don't think they'd be too keen to relive the last happy family outing before his accident.'

'Because it wouldn't be the same without Lenny?'

'Exactly.' I took a few deep, calming breaths and watched the TV – waiting for Arnold to change the subject.

'Exactly,' he said.

'What?' At first I thought he was mimicking me but the innocent expression on his face told me otherwise.

'Nothing is the same without Lenny, right?' Arnold said. 'Life has changed for ever for all of you and it's really sad. But if you never do anything together that you did with Lenny then you'll never do anything together ever again.' He let that idea sink in for a moment then continued. 'Maybe if you all missed him together it wouldn't be as bad as missing him alone. You might even realise you can still have fun together.'

I stared at the TV, thinking about Arnold's idea. The more I thought about it, the more I started to think he might actually have a point. We'd spent almost a year trying not to mention Lenny even though his memory filled our house – our lives. We'd become almost paralysed by the fear of saying his name, as though admitting we missed him would emphasise the size of the hole he left behind. It was like not acknowledging he was dead meant we could pretend he wasn't. The trouble was that not talking about him made me miss him even more. And the constant pressure to not speak about him meant we'd begun to speak less and less.

Now we hardly spoke at all.

Arnold was right. Instead of ignoring Lenny's absence, maybe it was time to face it head on. Last season's home match against the Kestrels was the last happy occasion we'd ever shared as a family of five. Maybe this year's could be our first as a family of four.

Arnold was typing feverishly on his phone.

'What are you doing?'

'Looking for tickets. On eBay.'

'I bet there won't be any. Or they'll cost a small fortune.'

'You're wrong,' Arnold said at last. 'They cost a reasonable-sized fortune.' He turned the screen to show me.

'That's outrageous. I haven't got anywhere near that kind of money.'

I had a twenty in my wallet and about sixty pounds of saved birthday money in my room. Arnold kindly offered fifty pounds and seventeen pence, which was in his bank account. But, after searching loads of other websites, we realised that the price of five tickets was way outside our budget.

'We could busk at the train station for more money,' Arnold suggested.

'Can you sing?'

He shook his head.

'Play an instrument?'

Arnold shook his head again. 'But I can juggle oranges,' he said proudly.

'Really? How many?'

'Three. Sometimes. Two easily.'

'Great,' I said. 'Let's get down to the station. I'll be like the ringmaster. *Roll up, roll up. Come and see the Unbelievable Juggling Arnold – he will leave you amazed and astounded as he keeps three, yes three, oranges in the air some of the time. But he can definitely juggle two easily.*'

Arnold was looking at me uncertainly. 'Sarcasm, right?' he said.

'No way. People will pay good money to see a kid who may, or may not, be able to juggle three oranges. That's entertainment gold.'

Arnold now seemed to have realised that I was indeed

being sarcastic. He nodded sadly. 'I was just trying to help.'

I felt guilty but I didn't know what to say so I said nothing.

'It was probably a stupid idea anyway,' Arnold mumbled. 'Maybe we should just ring the ticket office at the stadium and ask if there are any tickets left.'

Now this was definitely a stupid idea. The game had been a sell-out for weeks, which is why the prices for second-hand tickets were so high. But I didn't want to crush Arnold's enthusiasm again so I nodded encouragingly.

He searched the number online and dialled.

'Oh hello, good morning,' he said at last. 'Do you have any tickets left for the rugby match tomorrow? – None at all? – Completely sold out?'

I made a disappointed face.

Arnold continued, 'You see my friend was really hoping to watch the match with his family— I know, but watching it on TV isn't the same— He came to see the Panthers beat the Kestrels last season with his whole family but the next day his twin brother was run over and killed.'

My mouth fell open and I slapped his arm with the back of my hand. 'You can't say that,' I whispered.

Arnold mouthed to me, 'She remembers reading about you in the paper.'

'The thing is,' he continued, 'his family hasn't done anything together since. They haven't even had a meal together because it would make his brother's absence too real. Every day that goes by his family is getting more and more distant. His sister is going to university next year and his parents barely communicate with each other as it is. If he doesn't do something to save them now, his whole family might break up.'

As I listened to Arnold I felt my chest getting tighter. I'd thought getting everyone to the rugby match would be a good way of showing them that I want us to do stuff together and talk about Lenny. The way Arnold described it, my family was on the verge of breaking up. And he was right. Everything he'd said was true. If I didn't get them to the match, we might not be a family for much longer.

Arnold was off the phone. 'The match is sold out.'

'Yeah – I gathered.'

'But they have a few seats they keep for VIPs – sponsors and that sort of thing. She said she won't know for sure until later today or even tomorrow morning if they've all been taken. Sometimes the sponsors don't use all their tickets. Normally they would sell any spares on a first come, first served basis but she thought you were such a worthy cause she'd ask her boss if it's OK to hold them for you. She's going to ring me back a bit later this afternoon.'

'How much are the tickets?'

'Face value – twenty quid each, I think.'

'That's amazing, Arnold. I could kiss you. Don't look so terrified, I'm not actually going to kiss you.'

We had a good few hours to kill until we heard back from
the lady in the ticket office. Arnold suggested playing in
the arcade at the seafront so we decided to head down
to the pier. The quickest way to the front was to cut across
Chambers Park so we turned left out of my house. When
we got to the zebra crossing I pressed the button and
waited. Arnold glanced both ways and stepped into the
road. He was halfway across before he realised I wasn't
next to him. He stopped and turned back.

'What are you waiting for?'

'The green man,' I said, nodding at the illuminated
red figure.

Arnold looked around. 'There's no traffic.'

'I'll wait, thanks.'

'I think it's safe to cross.'

'I know. I'd still prefer to wait.'

Without saying a word Arnold walked back towards me, stepped onto the pavement and stood by my side. The green man lit up almost immediately and we crossed the road in silence.

Ash and Tom were tossing a rugby ball to each other in the middle of Chambers Park so Arnold and I went over to say hello. As we approached I could hear Tom barking instructions.

'More energy, Ash,' he called. 'Really fire that ball back to me. Better. Stay on your toes. We can't be caught flat-footed if we're going to win the final. Games don't come any bigger than that, you know.'

'This sounds like a serious coaching session,' I said when Arnold and I were a few metres from Ash. 'You won yesterday then?'

'Seventeen–six.' As Ash replied, he turned and smiled and Tom's bullet-like pass hit him square on the back of the head.

'Focus, Ash. Focus!' Tom screamed, his voice reaching a piercing pitch.

'Don't worry, I'm OK,' Ash called back, rubbing his head. 'Thanks for your concern though.'

'I'm not sure Tom's taking this seriously enough,' I said.

Ash rolled his eyes. 'Tell me about it. I thought we were just coming out for a bit of gentle catching practice.

Instead I'm being given an intensive training session by Drill Sergeant Hubbard.'

'Isn't he too young to be in the army?' Arnold asked.

'Ash just means Tom acts like one most of the time,' I explained.

'I think you mean all the time,' Ash added. As he spoke he gave me a quizzical look as if to ask why I was with Arnold. I just smiled. Tom jogged over to join us.

'Hi, Arnold,' Tom said brightly. 'How's it going?'

'How is what going?'

Tom smiled. 'How's your day going?'

'Fine thanks. I'm staying with Leon.'

Ash and Tom both knew my mum's attitude towards having friends over and looked surprised by Arnold's announcement. During the awkward silence that followed I tried to think of something interesting about Arnold to help Ash and Tom get to know him.

'Arnold lives with foster carers,' I said. Immediately I regretted my choice of words. I'd have hated to be labelled like that – 'This is Leon. His twin brother was killed last year.'

Tom looked uncomfortable. He cleared his throat and said, 'I'm sorry. When did your parents pass away?' He winced at his own bluntness. As if moving onto a brighter note he said, 'Of course they may still be alive? Maybe they just abandoned you? Or I suppose you might have been taken into care because they weren't looking after you properly ...?' Tom just about squeezed out the last few words before awkward tension tightened his vocal chords to the point where he could no longer speak.

Arnold waited a beat then said, 'My dad died when I was nine. My mum isn't very well. She gets really depressed. She's too ill to look after me at the moment so I'm with foster carers until she gets better.' He nodded at the ball under Tom's arm. 'Can we play? How about me and Leon take on you and Ash?'

Ash and Tom turned to me. Instinctively I scanned the park.

'Your mum's not here,' Ash said reassuringly. 'No contact. You won't get hurt. I promise.'

'Game on,' I said.

'Let me warn you, Arnold,' said Tom with a grin. 'When it comes to rugby, Ash and I don't take any prisoners.'

Arnold screwed his face up. 'Prisoners?'

The match was much closer than I expected it to be. It turned out Arnold was pretty good at rugby. He passed the ball accurately and was able to spiral it into my arms from a good twenty yards away. He was quick too, probably even faster than Ash in a straight line. His only downfall – and ultimately the downfall for our team – was his shoes. His old Converse trainers had virtually no grip

on the greasy grass. Every time he had to change direction quickly he ended up skidding out of the game or
sliding into the splits or just falling flat on his back.

'Why don't we pause the game for a bit and you can
go back to Leon's and change your shoes?' Ash suggested
on one occasion when Arnold had ended up spreadeagled
on the ground.

'No thanks,' Arnold replied, getting to his feet gingerly.

'It won't take a few minutes,' I offered.

'I don't have any other shoes.'

We all glanced down at the tattered trainers on
Arnold's feet. The canvas was grubby and frayed. One big
toe was peeping out where the toecap had come away
from the sole, which flapped noisily when Arnold broke
into a sprint.

'You could borrow a pair of mine,' I said.

'Look I said no, OK?'

'But you're sliding around all over the shop,' said Tom.

'What shop?'

'What size feet have you got? I've got a pair of boots
in my bag you can borrow.'

Because Arnold's voice was normally so calm, the
outburst that came next was all the more surprising.

'I said I'm all right, all right?' he screamed so loudly
that a couple of dog walkers about fifty yards away
stopped and turned round to see who was shouting in

the park like a lunatic. 'If I wanted to change my shoes I would have agreed to your suggestion straightaway, wouldn't I? Coming up with different shoes I might borrow doesn't alter the fact that I'm quite happy with these trainers thank you very much. I don't care if you're offering me Leon's trainers or Tom's boots, the answer is still the same. I don't want to change my shoes.'

Tom and Ash looked at each other then me. Even Ash's dark complexion seemed to have drained a little.

'Sorry, Arnold,' I said. 'You haven't quite made yourself clear. Do you want to borrow some trainers or not?'

As Arnold's head snapped round and he fixed me with a fiery gaze, I clapped and did jazz hands. His expression softened and his mouth relaxed into a smile.

'Sorry,' he laughed. 'I did lose my temper a bit there, didn't I?'

There was relieved laughter all round and we went back to playing the game. Arnold slipped over a few more times but nobody made any comment on his footwear. After an hour or so everyone was exhausted so we decided to stop the game with Tom and Ash about five tries in the lead.

'Well played,' Tom said, taking a long swig from a water bottle he had stashed in a rucksack. 'You're really quick, Arnold. Good hands too.'

'Thanks,' Arnold replied, shaking Tom's outstretched hand.

Tom offered Arnold his bottle but Arnold shook his head.

'It's OK,' Tom urged. 'I've got plenty.'

'Oh, it's not that,' said Arnold pleasantly. 'I just don't want to catch any illness that might be transferred into my body through your saliva.'

Ash, who was mid-swig at the time, gagged and sprayed a mouthful of water all over me. 'Don't take it personally, Tom,' he laughed, wiping his mouth with the back of his hand. 'Tell it like it is, Arnold.'

'It's nothing personal,' said Arnold, apparently baffled by the amusement he'd caused. 'All sorts of bacteria lurk in saliva. I wouldn't share a bottle with any of you.'

'Good man,' Tom grinned, high-fiving Arnold. 'I like a guy who isn't afraid to speak his mind.'

'In that case, you're going to get along like a house on fire,' I laughed. 'If you want an honest opinion, just ask Arnold.'

'In that case,' said Ash, drumming his fingers on his chin. 'What do you think of Tom's haircut?'

'It's OK,' Arnold replied, shrugging. 'Although if it was longer it would hide the fact that his ears stick out so much.'

Ash laughed and Tom clutched his chest as if he'd been shot.

'My turn,' said Tom. 'What do you think of Ash's T-shirt?'

Arnold studied Ash's top, which was covered in a bright floral print. 'It's pretty. It reminds me of a pair of curtains – or a tea towel.'

Ash bowed theatrically as Tom applauded.

'Listen, Arnold and I are off to the pier,' I said. 'Fancy coming?'

'I can't,' Tom said. 'I'm supposed to be helping my dad clear out the garage.'

Ash shook his head. 'I've got a tennis lesson this afternoon.'

'OK,' I said. 'We'll catch you later. Come on, Arnold.'

As we crossed Chambers Park my mobile rang – it was my mum.

'Leon?' she sounded stressed.

'Hi, Mum.'

'Where are you?'

'Just by the park – with some kids from school. Ash and Tom and that.'

'I've just picked up a message from Dr Laughlin.'

My therapy session – I'd forgotten all about it! I felt like a cannonball had dropped into my guts.

'I was worried sick about you. You can't imagine the scenarios going through my head.'

'I totally forgot, Mum. I'm really sorry.'

'I thought something terrible had happened to you.'

'I'm fine, Mum. I just slept late and it slipped my mind. I'm sorry I worried you.'

'Where are you going now?'

'Starbucks then down to the pier for a bit.'

'Well, be careful. Don't talk to any strangers. And watch the roads. Cars drive way too fast down Carlton Hill.'

'I will. See you later.'

'Text me in an hour.'

'OK. Bye, Mum.'

As I ended the call we turned onto Shorecliff Drive and headed for Starbucks. We stood side by side scanning the sandwiches and muffins on display and I had this strange feeling. Something about the situation was incredibly familiar.

'Lenny and I used to come here all the time,' I said. 'He always used to play this silly game.' The memory washed over me like a wave – drenching me with happiness before retreating and sucking me hollow.

'What game?'

'You know how they ask for your name so they can call you when your order's ready?'

Arnold nodded.

'Well, Lenny always used to give them a false name. The sillier the better.'

'What for?'

'Just for a laugh. It's funny when they call out your made-up name, all serious. Let's try it.'

'But what if you give them a name and someone else in the café has that name? Then the other person would collect your order.'

'I think it's pretty unlikely the real Quentin Ponsonby-Smythe-Carruthers is here, don't you?'

'Who's Quentin Ponsonby-Smythe-Carruthers?'

'That was Lenny's favourite fake name. Well, that and Owen Ritchie.'

'Why's that funny?'

'He's a famous rugby player. Probably the star of the whole Panthers team.'

'Will we see him play tomorrow?' Arnold asked.

I shook my head. 'Even if we do get tickets. He injured his shoulder a couple of weeks ago. He'll be out of action for a few months.' I nodded towards the lady at the till. 'Come on, let's order.'

Arnold chose a ham and cheese panini with a strawberry milkshake and I had a chicken wrap and a juice. A middle-aged woman took our order and my money without a smile or a 'thank you'.

'Name?' she said to Arnold.

Arnold looked at me and I gave him a small nod of encouragement. Then he smiled sweetly at the lady and said, 'Owen Ritchie the famous rugby player.'

She peered at him over her spectacles then wrote the name on the brown paper bag his panini was in.

'Are you having your wrap toasted?' she said to me wearily.

I nodded. Smiled.

'Name?' she sighed.

I could feel Arnold watching eagerly – waiting to hear the amusing fake name I'd come up with. The thing was I didn't have one ready. I'd never given a false name for anything. I'd only egged on Lenny when he did it. Suddenly in the spotlight the only name that came into my head was Quentin Ponsonby-Smythe-Carruthers. But I wanted to entertain Arnold with an amusing name of my own.

'My name?' I said, stalling.

The woman raised her eyebrows impatiently.

You don't realise how hard it is to make up a name on the spot until you actually have to do it. Try it for yourself. Just make up a funny random name right now. See what I mean? It's almost impossible.

My eyes darted about as I desperately ransacked my brain for a suitable name. I noticed some yellow goo oozing from a sandwich in the giant toaster on the counter.

'Cheese,' I blurted out at last. Wait, was that even a name? 'Cheeseman.' I knew that definitely was a name – the name belonging to the kindly tramp I'd befriended and taken home for tea some months previously.

'Really?' she sneered. 'You're going with Cheese Cheeseman?'

'No.' I laughed awkwardly. 'Just Cheeseman. Mr Cheeseman.'

While we waited for our snacks to be toasted, Arnold and I sat at a nearby table. He mentioned he needed to pop to a bank to get his money for the tickets and we were just working out where the nearest one was when someone shouted, 'Owen Ritchie!'

A kid who was not much older than me was holding up a paper bag and looking around the café. 'Owen Ritchie?' he said again.

Arnold didn't move. Looked at the kid blankly.

'That's you,' I whispered.

'Oh, right.' Arnold jumped to his feet 'Yes. That's me – Owen Ritchie.'

Stepping forward he took the sandwich.

Just as Arnold sat back down at our table, the kid called out, 'Cheeseman? Chicken wrap for Mr Cheeseman.'

I wanted to stand up and get my wrap straightaway because I felt sorry for the kid. But Arnold whispered to me to sit tight.

'Mr Cheeseman!' the kid called, sounding cross.

I couldn't bear it any more. Ignoring Arnold urging me to keep quiet, I got up to collect my wrap. I hadn't even noticed the figure dressed in a scruffy parka coming out of the toilets.

'Mr Cheeseman,' the kid repeated.

'Who's askin'?' said the man in the parka, squinting suspiciously at the kid.

'I've got a chicken wrap here for Mr Cheeseman,' the kid said, handing a paper bag to the man.

'Oh right,' the man remarked, sounding surprised. 'That's just the ticket. Nice one.'

As the man left with my lunch I caught the eye of the lady at the till. She was smiling triumphantly.

'That man's stolen your lunch,' said Arnold, getting to his feet.

'I know,' I replied. 'Come on.'

I followed the man outside and watched him delve into the bag and hungrily bite into my wrap.

'Hello, Mr Cheeseman!' I said.

'Leon!' The old man beamed. A piece of mayonnaisey chicken hung from his wiry beard. 'How are you doin', you little ratbag?'

'Fine, thank you. How are you?'

'Good as gold!' he grinned, showing off a mouth of yellow, mossy teeth. 'The weirdest thing just happened to

106

me. I only nipped into this café to use the gents' and on my way out that pasty little kid handed me a toasted chicken wrap with my name on it. Literally. How weird is that?'

'Really weird,' I agreed.

'How's school anyway?'

'Good.'

'And your family? Only this morning I was telling the boys at the bus depot about your mother's *coq au vin* – it really was the business.'

'I'm sorry they wouldn't let you stay. They can be a bit precious sometimes.'

Mr Cheeseman waved away my apology. 'They were just thinking of your safety. To be honest, I'd have been pretty concerned if they'd let an old drunk like me stay in their house just like that. How's life with you anyway? You here on your tod?'

'I'm OK thanks, Mr Cheeseman. This is my new friend, Arnold.'

Mr Cheeseman looked confused. 'Is Arnold your ... *imaginary* friend?' he asked at last.

'Of course not!' I laughed. 'This is Arnold.' But as I turned to indicate who Arnold was, I realised that Arnold was nowhere to be seen. 'Oh. Well, he was with me in Starbucks. I don't know where he's got to.'

'It's nothing to be ashamed of,' Mr Cheeseman said. 'I used to have an imaginary friend too. Big fella he was

– by the name of Tiny. Mind you Tiny never left me in the lurch like this Arnold geezer. You want to pick your imaginary friends more carefully.'

'I didn't make him up,' I laughed. 'He was right behind me when I saw you just now. I don't know where he is but...'

At that moment Arnold came out of the café.

'Arnold!' I said. 'There you are.'

'I know,' Arnold replied. 'Here I am.'

'Where have you been?'

Arnold shrugged. 'I was just getting a couple of napkins.'

'I see,' I said, as if some complex mystery had just been explained. 'Mr Cheeseman was starting to think I'd imagined you.'

Arnold glanced at Mr Cheeseman, then back to me. 'Imagined me doing what?'

'No. I mean made you up. Out of thin air.'

'Like my friend Tiny,' added Mr Cheeseman helpfully. 'He was a giant of a kid who lived in my head when I was a boy.'

If Arnold had been a cartoon he would have had steam pouring out of his ears at this point. 'How did a giant kid fit inside your head?' he asked.

'Never mind all that,' I said. 'I want you to meet a good friend of mine. Arnold, this is Mr Cheeseman.'

'All right, Arnold,' Mr Cheeseman said.

Arnold ignored the tramp's outstretched hand. 'You have chicken in your beard,' he said.

Mr Cheeseman picked the chicken off his beard and popped it into his mouth.

Then Arnold wrinkled up his nose. 'Something smells really bad out here.'

'Guilty as charged,' said Mr Cheeseman sheepishly. 'I'm afraid the spa at the Bus Depot Shangri-La is out of action at the moment.'

'Can't you complain to the manager?' Arnold asked, feeding a string of mozzarella into his mouth.

Mr Cheeseman looked at me.

'It's not an actual hotel,' I said. 'Mr Cheeseman sleeps rough round the back of the bus depot.'

'Is that why your clothes are so tatty?'

Mr Cheeseman chuckled. 'You don't mince your words, do you, son?'

Arnold shook his head. 'Have you always been home-less?'

Mr Cheeseman laughed a bit but then looked sad. 'No indeed, Arnie. Do you mind if I call you Arnie?'

'I prefer Arnold.'

Mr Cheeseman smiled. 'Well, Arnold, I used to have a house and a home and a family.'

'What happened to them?'

The tramp looked at the pavement. 'I was a stupid old git, that's what. I'm ashamed to admit I fell under the spell of a genie in a bottle.'

Arnold leaned towards me and whispered, 'What's he talking about? There's no such thing as genies. I think he's crazy.'

'He means alcohol,' I whispered.

Mr Cheeseman continued. 'I used to be a policeman. I started drinking every day – not when I was on duty but always afterwards. I'd stop on the way home and have a few pints. Soon I'd have a few shorts too and I'd keep going when I got home. I couldn't help myself. One night I was pulled over by my colleagues because I was driving all over the road. I lost my drivers' licence so I lost my job. Without my job I couldn't pay the mortgage on our house so my family lost its home. My wife went to live with her mother. She kicked me out and told me I could come back when I'd sobered up. That was five years ago.'

'Leon's family is about to break up,' announced Arnold. 'His parents avoid spending time together as a family. They don't even eat together.'

Mr Cheeseman looked horrified. 'Is that so?'

I nodded sadly. 'I think they're afraid to admit Lenny's not around. It's easier if they're on the move. If we're all spread out it's less obvious there's only four of us now.'

'But you have to spend time together,' Mr Cheeseman said. 'That's what being a family is all about.'

'We're going to get them all tickets to the rugby tomorrow,' said Arnold.

'We're going to try,' I added.

'Do you think they'll want to go?' Mr Cheeseman asked.

I shrugged. 'We'll have to trick them into meeting at the same place. I just hope once we've got them there – and have tickets – they'll see how important this is to me. And to all of us.'

Mr Cheeseman squeezed my shoulder. 'Good luck, Leon. If there's anything I can do to help, just let me know.'

He dug his hand deep into the pocket of his coat and produced a crumpled business card. Its edges were torn and it was stained with something unpleasant and brown but I could just about make out the faded lettering.

HARRY CHEESEMAN
DETECTIVE INSPECTOR

The mobile number printed beneath his name had been scored out with biro and another number had been scrawled underneath.

'If there's anything I can do to help – just call,' he

offered. 'If I'm not in the office, just leave a message with my assistant.'

'Office?' Arnold repeated.

Mr Cheeseman winked. 'There's a payphone by the depot. If I don't answer it, one of the other hotel residents will.'

I was thanking the tramp for his offer when Arnold asked, 'How are you going to help Leon's family? You can't even stop drinking for your own family.'

'I will.' Mr Cheeseman replied defiantly. From his pocket he produced a small glass bottle wrapped in brown paper, unscrewed the cap and took a long swig. 'After I've finished this bottle.' He smiled sadly. 'Mind you, I've been saying that for five years too.' Looking up at the clear blue sky he shook his head. 'It's going to be another cold one tonight, boys. I do hope the hotel maid has made up my bed with a winter duvet or I'm going to be frozen like a polar bear when the sun goes down.'

'What a waste,' I said, as I watched Mr Cheeseman weave his way down the street.

'I know,' Arnold agreed. 'Why don't you get another wrap? I'll wait.'

I turned and studied his blank face. 'I didn't mean it's a waste of my wrap. Do you remember the story about him losing his job, his house and his family?'

'Yeah?'

112

'*That's* a waste.'

'Oh right.'

'Weird though,' I said thoughtfully.

'What is?'

'I brought him home for tea a while back and my mum made him *boeuf bourguignon*.'

'Why's that so weird?'

'He was just saying how much he enjoyed my mum's *coq au vin*.'

'Maybe his memory's going?' Arnold suggested. 'Not surprising with all the drinking.'

'Hmmm.' I nodded. 'By the way – and this is not meant as a criticism. More of an observation really. I mean I'm no expert by any means so ...'

'Get on with it,' Arnold said.

'Well, I was thinking you could have been a bit more tactful about the smell.'

'I didn't know it was coming from him, though. I thought something had died.' Arnold jogged a few steps ahead and turned to face me. 'Why didn't you tell him about the chicken in his beard anyway?'

'I don't know. I didn't want to embarrass him, I suppose.'

'Wouldn't it be more embarrassing for him to go around all day with food on his face?'

I didn't have a good answer to that so I changed the

subject. 'And I think it would have been more polite just to thank him for offering to help us – instead of scoffing at the idea.'

'It was a crazy suggestion, though. How is he supposed to help anyway?'

'I don't know.' I made a quizzical face. 'But even when you think someone has said something ridiculous, you don't have to tell them so. It's sometimes more polite just to nod and say something like, "That's an interesting idea," or "I'll bear it in mind". Or even just say nothing. That way they'll think you're taking them seriously even though you've already dismissed what they said as utter rubbish. It's kinder that way.'

Arnold looked thoughtful for a moment. Then he smiled and said, 'That is an interesting idea.'

'I'm just trying to help,' I said.

'I know.' Arnold nodded. 'I'll bear it in mind.'

I needed the loo so I nipped back into the café. When I came out Arnold was exactly where I'd left him, staring at the sky.

'Do you still want to go to the arcade?' I asked.

'Yeah,' Arnold said and we started walking together. 'We can spend some of the money in the wallet.'

'I thought you said you didn't have any money.'

'I didn't. But I do now.'

'How come?'

'A man just gave it to me.'

'A man just gave you some money?'

'No. Why would a man just give me some money? That would be too weird.'

'I know.'

'So why did you suggest it?'

'Because you just said a man gave it to you.'

'That's right.'

'I'm confused. Did a man give you some money or not?'

'Yes and no.'

I stopped walking. Arnold stopped too and I gave him a serious stare. He seemed to know I was being serious because he swallowed slowly and pursed his lips.

'OK,' I said slowly. 'Imagine I'm a total idiot...'

'That won't be too hard.'

'Very funny. Imagine I'm a total idiot and explain to me as simply as you can how you had no money when we left my house but you do now.'

Arnold nodded seriously. 'So – when you were in the toilet a man came up to me and handed me this wallet.'

Arnold held up a black leather wallet like a referee showing a yellow card.

'Out of the blue?'

'The blue what?'

'Did he say anything?'

'Yes.'

I waited. Arnold blinked.

'Well?'

'Fine thanks.'

'I don't mean *are you well?*' I was starting to get frustrated. 'I mean *well, what did he say?*'

'Oh, right.' Arnold rolled his eyes towards the sky. 'As he was walking past, he stopped and picked up this wallet which was on the pavement, right by my feet. He handed it to me and said, "Excuse me, son – I think you've dropped your wallet."'

'What did you do then?'

'I took it off him.'

'Was it your wallet?'

Arnold looked confused. 'No.'

'So why didn't you tell the man it wasn't yours?'

'Well, he seemed so sure it was mine, I thought it would be more polite to say nothing.'

'We have to hand it in,' I said. 'We'll go past the police station on the way to the arcade.'

Arnold looked disappointed. 'It's got loads of money in it.'

'We can't take the money, Arnold. It's not ours.'

'Not even some of it?'

I shook my head.

'What about the tickets?' he asked. 'Can we keep them?'

'What tickets?'

Arnold beamed eagerly. 'Six tickets to the rugby match tomorrow.'

12

I knew it would have been wrong to take the tickets. That was a no-brainer. The tickets belonged to someone else. Fact.

'Show me,' I said.

From a black leather wallet Arnold produced the tickets – about the size of five-pound notes. He fanned them out like a game-show host showing off a cash prize. I reached for them then withdrew my hand sharply. I knew if I held them it would have been even more difficult to do the right thing and hand them in.

'Where are the seats?' I asked.

'Aren't they all in the stadium?' Arnold frowned. 'Facing the pitch?'

'I mean which block and what row?'

He peered at the tickets. 'Block twenty. Row P. Seats fifteen to twenty.'

That was pretty much bang on the halfway line. My first thought was *Lenny is going to be stoked!* How long before my brain stopped playing this cruel trick on me? The false joy of that idea was short-lived. Immediately my mind lurched into reality – *Lenny would have been so stoked*. That thought was pure sadness, dipped in regret and rolled in anger.

'We can't keep them,' I said, anger leaking into my voice.

'Why not?'

'Because they're not ours.' It had also occurred to me that whoever they belonged to might go to the stadium for the match and explain they'd lost their tickets and it would be really embarrassing if they found my family sitting in their seats. Getting thrown out of the ground was hardly the sort of experience I was hoping for. I didn't mention this to Arnold though because I was quite enjoying the view from the moral high ground.

'Can we at least take some of the money then?' he asked.

'No, Arnold. That's not ours, either.'

Arnold peered into the wallet. 'There's loads in here. We could take enough for the tickets and no one would notice.'

'That would be stealing,' I said. 'Anyway, we've got enough money for the tickets. If they're available. Has that lady from the ticket office rung you yet?'

Arnold checked his phone. Shook his head.

'Never mind. It's still early. Let's hand in the wallet then go to the arcade.'

It was only a few minutes' walk to the police station and Arnold spent the whole time complaining about handing in the wallet. As far as he could see, the man telling him it was his wallet meant that it was his wallet. Arnold seemed to think that was a much stronger argument than the fact that he knew for sure it wasn't his wallet.

He was still muttering in protest as we approached the drab concrete slab that was the local police station. The door had a panel made of glass, reinforced with a crisscross of wires. Something had punched a spider's web of cracks into the bottom corner. I pushed open the door and we approached the desk.

'What can I do for you two troublemakers then?' asked the desk sergeant. She had a square chin and thick eyebrows, one of which was raised. Her hair was black and cut in a straight fringe. She reminded me of a Lego figure.

'We haven't made any trouble,' said Arnold.

'We found a wallet,' I said.

The sergeant leaned her elbows on the desk. Her arms, which were folded, were fat and pink like two joints of ham. 'Well, well,' she said, shaking her head. 'Where did you find it?'

Arnold and I exchanged a glance.

'Just in Chambers Park,' I said sort of shrugging vaguely. I don't know why I lied. There was something about the sergeant's uniform and her stern expression that made me feel weirdly guilty – like I had something to hide. It just seemed less suspicious to have found a wallet full of money in a field rather than some man giving it to Arnold. My answer would have been perfectly believable too if, at exactly the same time, Arnold hadn't said, 'A man gave it to me.'

The sergeant's second eyebrow rose to join the first near the top of her forehead. She straightened up and looked down at us, her chins multiplying as her mouth opened.

'Come on now, lads,' she said. 'Which is it to be? Did you find the wallet in the park or did someone give it to you?'

'Oh, yeah,' I said, acting like I'd only just remembered what actually happened. 'That's right. Someone gave it to us.'

The tip of the sergeant's tongue popped out of her mouth as she scribbled some notes on a pad.

'Have you looked inside it?' she asked, looking up from her notes.

I felt my heart racing again. 'We may have glanced inside,' I said, waving a hand as if to suggest it was barely worth mentioning.

Arnold nodded. 'There's three hundred and fifteen pounds in cash, a credit card, a debit card, a dry-cleaning ticket and a Starbucks loyalty card. Oh, and six tickets to the rugby match tomorrow – block twenty, row P, seats fifteen to twenty.'

The sergeant turned to me and puffed out her cheeks. 'Sounds like someone *glanced* inside very thoroughly indeed.'

I smiled and swallowed hard.

The sergeant glared at me and when she spoke her voice came out burbling with menace. 'Do you have any idea how long you can go to prison for lying to a police officer?'

I felt the blood drain from my cheeks – but before I could answer the sergeant winked at me. 'Don't look so worried, laddie – I'm only kiddin' you on. You're not exactly the Kray twins now, are you?'

I managed a smile and a relieved laugh escaped my mouth.

'We're not even brothers,' Arnold offered sincerely.

'I'll let you into a little secret,' the sergeant whispered. 'I'm not as scary as I look. This uniform makes me seem way stricter than I really am. Underneath this official exterior I'm just a normal lady, so just relax. Truth is I like you two lads. You're doing something good here today. If everyone was as honest as you two, the world would be a much better place.'

122

Arnold and I gave our names (our real ones) and mobile numbers. The police officer told us her name was Sergeant McIntosh. Arnold explained in more detail about how he'd been waiting for me outside Starbucks when a man had noticed the wallet on the floor, picked it up and handed it to him.

'Did it occur to you to tell him it wasn't your wallet?' Sergeant McIntosh asked.

Arnold shook his head. 'Leon told me it was more polite to just say nothing – even if you know someone is talking rubbish.'

I smiled awkwardly. 'That advice made a lot more sense at the time.'

'I'm sure it did,' Sergeant McIntosh smiled and made some more notes. 'When you *glanced* inside the wallet, did you happen to see the name on the bank cards?'

'Mr C. J. Miller,' said Arnold.

'And you didn't think to ask in Starbucks whether Mr Miller was inside – unaware that he'd dropped his wallet?'

I realised that would have been a pretty smart thing to have done. 'No,' I said. 'Sorry.'

She scribbled some more. 'What happens now?' I asked.

'Now?' Sergeant McIntosh puffed out her cheeks again. 'Now I'll call one of my constables to take you down to the torture chamber.'

I knew immediately Sergeant McIntosh was winding

us up again and I smiled at her joke. She tried her best to keep a straight face, but when she saw the look of horror on Arnold's face she burst into hysterical laughter.

'What's so funny?' Arnold asked.

'The look on your face, laddie,' Sergeant McIntosh wheezed, her round cheeks bright pink now. Wiping a tear from her cheek she continued, 'I'm sorry. That was a wee bit cruel. There aren't many laughs working in a place like this, but that was a good one.'

Arnold waited until the police officer's laughter had stopped. 'Seriously,' he said...seriously. 'What happens now?'

'Right, yes,' Sergeant McIntosh stood up straight and laced her fingers together on the desk. 'Seriously – we will contact Mr Miller and tell him his wallet has been handed in to us. I'm sure he'll be extremely grateful to you both.'

'Do you think there will be a reward?' Arnold asked boldly.

'A reward?' Sergeant McIntosh raised her thick eyebrows. 'Possibly, I don't know. I suppose it depends how grateful Mr Miller is to you both.'

I nodded, feeling slightly awkward about asking for a reward. After all that wasn't the reason we'd handed in the wallet in the first place. But I wasn't surprised that Arnold was feeling none of my discomfort.

'If he does want to thank us,' he pressed. 'Could you ask if we can have his tickets to the rugby match tomorrow? We only need five, actually, so he could keep one.'

'I'm not sure he's going to be *quite that* grateful,' Sergeant McIntosh chuckled. 'I was thinking he might be grateful to the tune of about ten quid each.'

'Oh,' Arnold replied. 'I don't think I know that tune?'

'Both keen rugby fans, are you?' Sergeant McIntosh enquired.

I nodded.

'Leon and his twin Lenny used to play in their school rugby team together. But Lenny was killed a year ago and Leon's mum won't let him play any more.'

'Slightly more information than Sergeant McIntosh was expecting,' I muttered.

'I'm sorry to hear that, Leon,' Sergeant McIntosh said. 'My brother and I used to play rugby in the garden when we were kids. He went on to play at a much higher level than me but I like to think I taught him everything he knows.'

The police officer smiled and winked at me. I nodded gratefully.

A few minutes later Sergeant McIntosh had finished filling out her paperwork on the wallet and told us we were free to go. She thanked us again for our honesty and wished us a safe afternoon.

'I'll contact you if anything comes up in the reward department,' she said as I pulled open the door with the spider's web crack. 'But don't hold your breath.'

It was a relief to get outside into the cold fresh air after the stuffy police station.

'Why would we hold our breath?' Arnold asked. 'We'd suffocate within about five minutes, then the reward would be no good to us.'

'I don't know,' I said, taking a deep breath. 'Come on then.'

'Come on what?'

'Last one to the pier's a loser.' I tapped Arnold's chest with the back of my hand and legged it.

13

I could hear the loose sole on Arnold's shoe flapping behind me as I pelted across the paved avenue leading up to the pier. The sky was clear and a salty breeze was blowing my hair off my forehead. Lenny and I used to race everywhere. He was always faster than me – but only just. Mum didn't like me running anywhere now because, 'You're not careful enough if you're charging around...' But it felt good racing Arnold. Not because I was faster than him. There was just something pure and natural about running as fast as you can.

I slapped my hand on the wall next to the entrance to the arcade. Arnold staggered to a halt next to me and doubled over.

'I win,' I gasped, pinching my sides. 'You're a loser.'

'You had a head start,' he said, beaming.

'If you snooze you lose.'

Arnold crouched down to inspect his trainers. The loose sole had come away even further now. When he pulled the toecap up I could see all his toes inside the thick green sock.

'Let's see if we can win some money on the slots,' I suggested.

Arnold nodded eagerly. 'I love playing the fruit machines.'

He led me into the arcade. The atmosphere inside was totally different to the wide-open peacefulness outside. It was dark and crowded and noisy. I followed Arnold past rows of people standing in front of machines. Eagerly feeding coins into slots or staring intently at screens, they seemed mesmerised. Garish lights flashed in the gloom, briefly lighting their zombie-like faces. Joysticks rattled and bells rang and levers cranked and coins *kerchinged*.

We went straight to the cashier. I had a five-pound note left from my twenty, which I changed into ten-pence pieces. Even if we lost the lot we'd still have enough money between us to buy the tickets – if they were available. I followed Arnold as he prowled the arcade in search of a free fruit machine.

'Here's one!' I said, raising my voice above the *whoo-whoo-whoo* coming from a pinball machine.

Arnold shook his head. 'Not that one,' he said. We rounded the corner and he pointed to a fruit machine being played by an old lady in a smart red coat and black felt hat. 'We want to play that one.'

'Why don't we just play one of these?' I asked, nodding at the free machines further along the row. Arnold shook his head. Folding his arms he stood right behind the old lady, like he was queuing to use a cash machine. 'Nine is my lucky number and this is the ninth machine in this row.'

Glancing to his right Arnold spotted something that made him grab my wrist. He nodded towards a large figure strolling towards us. 'Here comes the security guard,' he said from the corner of his mouth. 'Just act natural.'

Acting natural was exactly what I had been doing. In fact, acting natural had seemed like the most...well, natural thing in the world to do. Right up to the point where Arnold told me to act natural. From that moment on, I discovered that acting natural was the most impossible thing in the whole world.

I tried folding my arms but for some reason they kept coming unfolded. Hands on hips felt too aggressive – like I was waiting for a scrap. I tried leaning casually against a fruit machine but it was further away than I'd anticipated so I ended up stretched out at about forty-five degrees to the floor. When I tried to stand upright again I pushed too hard on the machine and it rocked back slightly. Unfortunately it was the exact moment the security guard was passing right behind me.

'Don't lean on the machines, sunshine,' he said threateningly.

'Sorry, officer,' I said.

'I'll be watching you,' he said, pointing at his eye – presumably in case I didn't know which organ he'd be using to watch me.

'Sure.' As I spoke, I recognised the guard's chubby hamsterish face. 'You're Greg Watkins.' What I didn't say was, *you used to bully me at school because I was younger and studious and you thought education was for losers.*

'Who are you?' he said, narrowing his already tiny eyes.

Arnold and I exchanged the briefest of glances. 'Cheeseman,' I said quick as a flash. Greg looked dubious for a moment and I thought I'd been rumbled but then he nodded. 'Ahh yes I remember you, Cheeseman. You were in Dunphy's class, weren't you?'

'Mitchel's' I said, feeling a strange thrill at my deception.

'That's right.'

'So you work here now?'

Greg hooked his thumbs into his belt and puffed out his belly. 'Yup,' he said proudly. 'Assistant Security Officer and Crime Prevention Technician.' As he spoke his throat seemed to inflate like a bullfrog's.

'Cool,' I said looking around in awe like I was in the Sistine Chapel, or something. 'Good for you. Who needs GCSEs, right?'

Greg smiled smugly. 'If I work hard, in ten years I might make it to the top.'

'Wow,' I said.

'The top of what?' Arnold asked.

Greg tilted his head back slightly. 'I'll be Head of Security and Crime Prevention.'

'What does that mean?' Arnold probed.

Greg smirked and patted his left shoulder with his right hand. 'It means I'll get four gold stripes instead of two. And a cap.'

I could tell Arnold was going to ask what difference having a cap to wear would make so I said loudly, 'That's really brilliant.'

'Anyway,' Greg said sternly, 'like I said, I'll be watching you.'

Arnold and I watched him waddle away.

'What's the big deal about a new hat?' Arnold wondered aloud.

For fifteen minutes we waited in silence, watching the old lady scooping coins out of a plastic cup and feeding them into the slot. When she got down to her last couple of coins, Arnold turned to me and whispered, 'Get ready.'

I didn't really know how I was supposed to 'get ready' for playing a fruit machine. It wasn't the sort of thing that you needed to warm up for or anything. I decided to do some little jumps on the spot just to show how eager I was.

With her next coin the lady got two cherries and a plum. Lights flashed and a bell rang and coins started cascading out of the machine into the little scoop at the bottom. She turned and grinned at Arnold then punched the air, like a footballer celebrating a goal. I stopped jumping up and down.

For another ten minutes we watched the old lady feeding the fruit machine until, at long last, her plastic cup was empty and she shuffled away.

'OK,' said Arnold, sliding a coin into the slot. 'Let's see how we can do.'

'Yeah,' I said, looking over his shoulder. 'Let's see if Mr Jack and Mr Pot are coming out to play.'

'Who?' Arnold turned to face me.

'Mr Jack and Mr Pot,' I said, already wishing I hadn't started. 'You know – as in "jackpot". I meant let's see if we can win the jackpot. I realise I should have just said that in the first place. Sorry.'

Arnold accepted my apology with a short nod, turned back to the fruit machine and pulled on the lever. We watched the blur of fruit as the drums started spinning. As they clicked to a standstill in turn I held my breath. My eyes swept along the win line, expecting to see three jackpot symbols, which would mean we'd won. The jackpot. Obviously.

I checked the pictures again. Compared them to the pictures of winning combinations plastered all over the machine. Plum, cherry, jackpot symbol.

I exhaled with a sigh.

Nothing. Not even a free spin.

Arnold groaned and slid in another coin. He pulled the handle and the drums whirred round. Click, click, click they stopped. My eyes scanned the win line.

'Lemon, lemon, fireman's helmet,' I said. 'What do we win for that?'

'It's a bell, not a fireman's helmet,' Arnold replied. 'And it's worth nothing.'

'I thought this machine was a sure-fire winner?' I mumbled.

'Trust me,' Arnold said, cranking down the handle again. 'You just have to be patient.'

By the time the machine had swallowed £4.80 of our fiver I had resigned myself to the fact that we weren't destined to win the jackpot after all. Over the tops of the rows of fruit machines I could see the entrance and clear blue sky waiting beyond.

'Bingo!' Arnold exclaimed.

My eyes flashed back to the win line on his fruit machine.

Jackpot symbol, bell, jackpot symbol.

Excitedly I scanned the winning combinations displayed on the fruit machine, but I couldn't see a match for what we'd got. As my excitement faded it occurred to me that if we did have a winning combination, the machine would already be flashing and dinging and spewing out coins. It wasn't doing any of these things.

I looked at Arnold. 'You haven't won anything.'

'Not yet,' he said mysteriously. 'I still have three nudges.'

'Sure,' I said, waiting for Arnold to start nudging. But instead of tapping the nudge button, he stood still and closed his eyes.

'What are you doing?' I whispered.

'Working out whether to nudge up or down.'

'How?'

'I'm picturing the symbols on the middle reel,' Arnold replied without opening his eyes. 'I've memorised the sequence.'

'Shut up,' I laughed. 'There must me about twenty symbols on each drum.'

'Thirty-two actually.'

'And you memorised them as they were spinning round?'

Arnold opened his eyes and looked at me. 'Yup.'

I was dubious of Arnold's claim. It was almost impossible to see the symbols as they spun round, never mind memorise them.

'How did you know you'd need to remember the pictures on the middle reel?' I said.

'I didn't.' Arnold shrugged. 'I memorised all three of them.'

Arnold interlaced his fingers and stretched out his arms, cracking his knuckles. Then he tapped the nudge button with one finger. The middle drum clicked upwards onto the next symbol.

'Jackpot, pineapple, jackpot,' I muttered.

'Next should be Jackpot, plum, jackpot,' Arnold said. He tapped the nudge and the middle reel clicked round again.

He was right. A plum symbol appeared in the middle window.

'Get ready to celebrate,' Arnold murmured.

He tapped the nudge button.

I held my breath.

The middle drum clicked round.

Jackpot, jackpot, jackpot.

An electronic fanfare sounded and all the lights on the fruit machine started flashing. From below the main display a waterfall of silver coins started pouring out of the machine.

'You did it!' I whooped. 'That was amazing.'

Arnold dropped to his knees, catching the coins as they fell. I kneeled down next to him and helped. We both laughed as we scooped handfuls of coins into our pockets.

'Congratulations, lads.'

I recognised the security guard's voice, but there was something in his tone that made me uncomfortable. I stood up and turned to face him.

'Thanks,' I said.

'You must have about fifty quid in winnings there,' Greg said with a fixed smile. Arnold turned and stood next to me. Having filled his pockets he had resorted to using his sweatshirt as a sort of hammock into which he'd scooped the remainder of our winnings.

Arnold said, 'Fifty-three pounds and forty pence.'

'It's a shame really,' said Greg, his cheeks wobbling as he shook his head.

'What is?' I asked.

'You're both too young to gamble. I'll have to confiscate your winnings.'

'You can't do that,' Arnold protested.

'Yes I can, sonny.' Greg took a step towards Arnold. 'You're lucky I don't arrest you for illegal gambling.'

'It's OK,' I said, placing a reassuring hand on Arnold's arm. 'Greg's right. Good job, Greg. You've averted a major crime taking place here – I expect there'll be some sort of reward for you. Maybe a promotion – an extra stripe on your shoulder? That's probably why your boss is coming over – to congratulate you.'

I nodded towards an imaginary figure coming down the aisle behind the security guard. As Greg turned to greet his boss, I grabbed a fistful of Arnold's sweatshirt. Catching Arnold's eye I mouthed the word *run* and pulled him alongside me as I started for the exit.

'Hey!' Greg protested. Turning, I saw he was about ten yards back, his eyes wild and his fat cheeks flushed.

As we sped through the arcade, dodging people and darting this way and that to throw the guard off our tail, a constant trickle of coins fell from Arnold's makeshift pouch.

At one point we doubled back on ourselves in the hope of outfoxing Greg. Unfortunately we were too clever for our own good and just ended up face-to-face with him. In his surprise Arnold let go of his sweatshirt and a whole pile of coins dropped to the floor where they scattered like a shattered vase. Greg seemed unsure whether his priority was to grab us or the coins and we took advantage of his moment's indecision by turning and scarpering.

Eventually we burst out of the arcade into the freedom of broad daylight. Laughing aloud we sprinted along the pier with Arnold's dodgy shoe slapping an offbeat rhythm on the wooden decking.

14

When we reached the end of the pier we turned to see if anyone had followed us. There was no sign of Greg's ripe cheeks amongst the relaxed faces of people enjoying a stroll in the autumn sunshine.

My heart was still pounding like crazy. Partly because of the physical effort of running away and partly because I was terrified of getting caught.

'Looks like the coast is clear,' I said.

Arnold turned and surveyed the beach. 'Clear of what?'

'I mean it doesn't look like Greg is chasing us any more.'

'Oh right. No – I think we got away with it.' Arnold patted his bulging pockets and they chinked.

'Fancy an ice cream?' I said, nodding at a kiosk on the pier.

Arnold nodded eagerly. 'I could kill a Cornetto.'

'You mean you could murder a Cornetto,' I laughed.

'Either way, it's my treat.'

I chose a Mint Magnum and Arnold went for a strawberry Cornetto. The lady selling the ice creams looked at Arnold suspiciously when he emptied two handfuls of ten-pence coins onto the counter.

'He's just raided his piggy bank,' I said sheepishly.

Tucking into our ice creams, we wandered to the very end of the pier. Arnold slid his legs under the bottom railing and hung his arms over it, sitting on the decking with his feet dangling over the edge. I copied him and we both gazed out to sea, eating in silence.

'I still can't believe we just did that,' I said, licking the last trace of ice cream off my lolly stick.

'It was your idea to run,' said Arnold.

'We won that money fair and square. I mean you did.'

'Do you think we'll be in trouble?' Arnold asked.

I shook my head. 'Nobody knows who we really are so they've got no proof how old we are.'

'But it's still illegal.'

'Look,' I said. 'How about we do something good with the money? If we give it to charity then it's not so bad, is it?'

'We could buy some blankets for Mr Cheeseman,'

Arnold suggested. 'He did say he'd be freezing sleeping outside tonight.'

'Now that,' I said, 'is a brilliant idea.'

I checked my phone to see if Olivia had texted me about the message I'd left. Nothing. But there was a message from my mum checking I was OK. I typed out a short reply to say I'd been in the arcade and was having an ice cream on the pier. I pressed send and slid my phone back into my pocket.

'So when are you going to tell your parents I'm staying?' Arnold asked.

I turned to him, but he just kept staring at the horizon so he didn't see the *I don't know what you're on about* expression on my face. Which was probably for the best because I wasn't very good at acting and Arnold wasn't very good at reading facial expressions.

Instead I tried to get my message across by saying, 'I don't know what you're on about.'

Arnold popped the tip of his Cornetto cone into his mouth and crunched it up.

'I know you were sneaking me into the house last night,' he said. 'Why else would you have asked me to go and wait by the front door? You didn't really think I believed all that stuff about your family tradition? I might be a bit strange but I'm not stupid.'

I tried to do an innocent face.

'You're a terrible actor, Leon Copeman.'

'Sorry,' I said, allowing my eyebrows to sink to their normal level. 'I would have told you the truth...eventually.'

'Why did you say I could come and stay in the first place?' Arnold asked, looking down at the sea slapping and frothing against the pier's sturdy wooden supports.

'Honestly?'

'Honestly.'

'I was only joking about you staying. I didn't know how to tell you I hadn't been serious. I sort of felt sorry for you.'

'So you let me come and stay out of pity?'

'I wouldn't say pity exactly,' I said with a shrug. 'I like helping people.'

'Because of what happened to your brother?' Arnold asked. 'You feel guilty about how he died so you try and make up for it by helping waifs and strays?'

'No,' I snorted. 'Sounds like you've been reading the Dummies' Guide to Psychobabble.'

'I don't know that book.'

'OK,' I confessed. 'Maybe I was trying to help you to make up for not helping Lenny.'

'So you said it was OK for me to stay even though you knew your mum would say no?'

142

'Uh-huh,' I said, looking away instinctively.

I expected Arnold to be angry but he said, 'That's pretty cool.'

'Is it?'

'Yeah – you took a risk for me. How do you think your mum will react when she finds out I'm staying in your room?'

An image of a nuclear mushroom cloud came into my head. 'I'm not sure,' I said.

'It's still a big risk for someone you don't even know.'

'Just because you don't know someone doesn't mean you shouldn't help them,' I said. 'Besides...' I didn't finish my thought because I wasn't sure if I wanted to share it.

'Besides ...?'

I looked at Arnold, sizing him up. His features were blunt and simple somehow, like he'd been moulded from clay by a kid. Even the locks of his hair looked like thinly rolled sausages. But there was something honest about his muddy-brown eyes. I already knew he had a tendency to speak his mind and I admired that about him. (I mean, it had been a bit of a shock at first but I'd got used to it.) Something told me I could trust him – I could tell him stuff I might keep from anyone else.

'Besides,' I began with an embarrassed smile, 'I thought it might give Lenny a kick.'

'Why do you want to kick Lenny?'

'It means he'd enjoy it,' I said. 'He was a bit of a tearaway – always breaking rules and giving me a hard time because I'm such a goody-goody. I like to think he's up there now,' I raised my eyes skywards. 'If he is watching me, he'd love seeing me breaking the rules like this. His squeaky-clean brother sneaking a kid into the house! He'd be absolutely killing himself.' Before Arnold could protest I said, 'That means he'd be laughing. A lot. I bet he's got tears rolling down his cheeks.'

'Like you do now?' Arnold said.

'That's just the wind making my eyes water,' I said, wiping my cheeks with the heel of my hand.

Arnold kicked his feet against the pier. His shoe flapped like a duck quacking.

'Why didn't you tell me all this?' he said. 'Instead of pretending it was all sorted?'

'No reason.' I thought about my answer for a moment – felt guilty about its deceit. I turned and held Arnold's gaze. 'OK, I didn't want you to think my parents were rejecting you. I thought that might make you feel worse, you know, about everything. About yourself.'

'What, so because my mum can't look after me I'm supposed to feel worthless?'

'I didn't know anything about your mum to start with,' I said, sort of hoping to change the subject.

'But now you do,' Arnold persisted. 'You think my self-esteem is so low that I might have felt rejected by your parents even though I'd never met them?'

I shrugged.

'Now who's been reading the Dummies' Guide to Psychobubbles?'

'Psycho*babble*,' I laughed. 'Sorry. It's a load of rubbish, isn't it?'

Arnold shook his head. 'Actually no,' he said quietly. 'You're right – my self-esteem can get really low. I mean I never feel great about myself. I know I'm a bit odd – I don't get jokes and stuff and I can be too blunt for some people – so I've never really had many friends. But when my mum couldn't handle me, it felt like the ultimate rejection. I mean, I know she's ill but it still hurts. Why can't she just be happy with me? It feels like I'm not enough for her. Sometimes I think I might be able to fix her – to cheer her up if I was a better person.'

I often have imaginary conversations. Sometimes I'm sort of rehearsing what I'd like to say one day – like asking my dad if we can try doing some of the stuff we used to do. Or telling Mum I understand that she blames me for Lenny's death. Other times I wonder what I'd say in weird situations. Like, the other day, I had this whole conversation in my head where Olivia's best friend was constantly telling her that her designs were rubbish.

I gave her this whole chat about what an amazingly talented girl she is and how she deserved better. I did a pretty good job too. By the end of my pep talk Olivia was going to start her own fashion label.

In all my daydream conversations, I've never imagined what I might say to a kid who's feeling responsible for his mum's depression.

My mouth hung slightly agape for a while. I've learned over the last year that saying nothing to someone who's sad is better than saying something dumb. Sometimes listening is better than talking. Most of the time actually.

'She's supposed to look after me,' Arnold said quietly. 'Since my dad died she's all I have left. It doesn't bother me if other people don't like me or don't want to spend time with me. They don't get me and that's fine. But she is my mum. It's her job to look after me. If I was more like other kids maybe she'd love me more and we'd be happy together.' Arnold's voice was steady and his facial expression barely changed. He just hung his head, looking down at his tatty shoes and the foaming water below.

'But she didn't choose not to look after you, did she?' I said. 'You said she was too ill – too depressed – to care for you.'

Arnold nodded. 'I know. But I can't help thinking she might be able to cope if I was more … *normal*.'

146

'What is normal anyway?' I said. 'You're special, Arnold. I'm sure your mum loves you for it.'

Arnold sighed and stared at the ocean.

'She must be in a really bad place,' I said.

Arnold shrugged. 'Portsmouth's not *that* bad.'

'I mean she must be so unbearably sad.'

Arnold nodded. 'She gets so down she can't summon up the energy to get out of bed for days. My counsellor says when people get as depressed as Mum gets, they can't see anything other than their own pain. He said it has nothing to do with how she feels about me – she's just sick and is struggling to get herself better.'

'Does hearing that make it any easier?'

Arnold looked thoughtful for a moment, then shook his head. 'It just makes me wish I could help her. I wish she'd try harder to feel happier. Sometimes I get frustrated with her and I wish I could be more understanding.'

I didn't have any words that could begin to address the emotions Arnold was feeling. What could I say that could make him feel better?

Instead of speaking, I put an arm round his shoulder and squeezed gently.

'What are you doing that for?' he said.

'I just want you to know I'm here.'

'I know you're here. You're right next to me.'

'I mean I'm your friend.'

'Oh, OK,' he said simply. 'As we're friends, you ought to know I'm not really that comfortable with physical contact.'

'Tough,' I said and squeezed him tighter.

15

After a while I let my arm drop and we sat in silence for a bit longer. I thought about how hard every day must be for Arnold. Sometimes when I woke up I'd feel sorry for myself. I wouldn't be sure if I'd be able to face the day – and I still had my family to help support me. OK, they may not have been perfect. Mum and Dad hardly spoke to each other and they were both terrified of mentioning Lenny to me so they did this awkward chitchat instead of normal conversations. And we never spent any time together any more because that would have just made it too obvious that Lenny was gone. But at least we were physically close. I mean we were in the same house, not always hugging and stuff.

Arnold was totally alone. It must have been hard enough for him to cope with his dad's sudden death but then his mum getting sick . . .

'Mum loved shoes,' Arnold smiled. 'She was always buying a new pair – drove my dad mad with them. When he complained about her spending too much money on shoes she'd just smile and quote this old Hollywood actress – Marilyn Monroe. *Give a girl the right shoes, and she can conquer the world.*

'After my dad's heart attack she started wearing the same pair of old boots every day. She thinks you can tell a lot about someone by what they have on their feet. She used to joke that her shoes were tired and sad just like her. Sometimes she'd talk about buying a new pair when she felt better … but she still hasn't.'

I glanced at Arnold's scruffy trainers and my expression must have changed somehow because Arnold said, 'What?'

'I think you deserve some new shoes,' I said.

Arnold gave me a serious look. 'I don't know what you mean.'

A seagull squawked overhead and a gust of wind whistled between the pier's wooden supports.

'I'm freezing,' I said brightly. 'Come on, it's much too cold for a dip today anyway. Let's go.' I clambered to my feet and held out a hand to Arnold. He took it firmly and pulled himself upright.

'Where are we going?'

'Well, we're bandits, aren't we?' I said, showing him

a handful of coins to emphasise the point. 'We shouldn't hang around the scene of the crime, should we? Let's make our getaway and spend our loot.'

'Eighty, ninety and ten makes forty pounds,' said Arnold, stacking up the ten pence pieces on the counter.

The army surplus store smelled musty. The shelves were crammed with piles of trousers and jackets in khaki and camouflage. There were helmets and berets and all sorts of belts and harnesses with loads of pockets for ammunition and stuff.

The shop assistant was dressed like a commando – head to toe in camouflage gear. His big belly overhung a thick webbing belt that boasted a holstered pistol on his right hip. He wore a black woollen hat rolled up so it sat on the top of his egg-like head. He'd even smeared that black war paint over his face for extra authenticity. Either that or he'd been changing the oil in his car.

'Have you two just emptied a slot machine, or something?' he asked, sounding like a Cornish pirate. I'd been expecting some comment so I'd planned a cover story. Actually it was the same line I'd used at the ice-cream kiosk about raiding a piggy bank. I was just drawing breath when Arnold said. 'Yes. Down at the arcade on the pier.'

The shop assistant's laugh was scarily loud. Then it

stopped suddenly and he leaned towards us with a piratical glint in his eye. 'I've often thought about going down there and *making a withdrawal* – if you get my drift, me hearties,' he leered. OK, he didn't say the *me hearties* bit, but he might as well have done.

'Really?' I said uncertainly.

The assistant peered over our heads like he was making sure no one else could hear what he was about to say. 'I've got it all planned out,' he whispered. 'I'd enter through the north entrance and make my way to the cashier's desk. The security guard patrols in a classic five-nine pattern so when he's at the southern corner I'd strike.'

'What would you do?' Arnold said.

The assistant patted the weapon in his belt. 'Tell them they've got twenty seconds to give me the money before it starts raining lead. I could waltz in and out of there in under a minute.'

'Wouldn't the waltzing be a bit weird?' Arnold asked.

The shop assistant looked confused.

'He just means he'd be really quick,' I explained to Arnold.

'Is the gun real?' I asked.

The assistant nodded proudly. 'It is a genuine replica of a bona fide Smith and Wesson point forty-five.'

'So it's like a toy?' Arnold said.

'It's not a toy,' the shop assistant said tetchily.

'Does it fire bullets?' Arnold asked.

The shop assistant shook his head.

'Sounds like a toy to me,' Arnold said.

The shop assistant pursed his lips. 'I can do you a special price on one.' He spun his pistol on one finger like a cowboy. Then he grabbed it by the barrel and offered it to me. 'Half price.'

'I'm thirteen,' I said, gently pushing the replica gun back towards the shop assistant. 'We really just want the blankets.'

The shop assistant placed his gun on the counter and said, 'OK, I understand. Not everyone can handle a piece like this anyway.'

The assistant started rolling his beanie hat down. As he pulled it over his face I realised it was a commando balaclava. It covered his entire head except for two elliptical holes for his eyes and a small circular hole for his mouth. It made him look instantly menacing – creepy even.

'Tell you what,' he said through the round hole. 'I'll throw in one of these for free.' Taking a balaclava off the shelf he tossed it onto the pile of blankets we were buying.

'Thanks,' Arnold said, snatching it up. He rolled it up into a beanie and pulled it onto his head.

'Come on,' I said. 'Let's go.'

Arnold was carrying a plastic bag containing a sandwich and a fizzy drink we'd bought in the newsagent's next door. He looped the handle over his wrist then we scooped up a pile of blankets each, thanked the shop assistant and headed out. The bell above the door rang as I opened it.

'If you change your mind about the point forty-five, you know where I am.' The assistant tapped where his nose would have been if he wasn't wearing a balaclava. 'Mum's the word.'

It had grown cold outside. The wind had picked up and people were walking with their heads ducked, holding onto caps. With the blankets tucked under our chins Arnold and I headed for the bus depot. The plastic bag bounced off Arnold's thigh with each step.

As expected we found Mr Cheeseman round the back of the bus depot, outside the toilets. He was lying on some cardboard boxes, which he'd flattened out into a makeshift mattress. Curled up on his side like a baby, he was wearing a bin liner over his jacket and clutching an empty bottle of whiskey like it was a teddy.

'Mr Cheeseman,' I said.

He didn't stir – didn't move a muscle.

I called his name a few more times, speaking louder each time. Nothing.

'Do you think he's all right?' I asked.

'No.' Arnold shook his head. 'I think he's really, really drunk.'

'I know he's drunk, you doughnut,' I said. 'I mean, do you think he's still alive?'

'Why didn't you just ask if I think he's still alive then?'

We studied him closely for any sign that he was breathing. I couldn't see any movement of his chest. There was no telltale flaring of his nostrils, either. I could feel my pulse start to quicken. If he was dead I would never be able to forgive myself. I would always blame myself for not standing up to my parents when they said he couldn't stay with us. His would be yet another death on my conscience – another occasion I would look back on and wish I'd acted differently. Another life I might have saved if I'd been braver and intervened sooner.

I placed my blankets on the floor and kneeled next to Mr Cheeseman's pathetic body. The concrete slabs were cold and hard on my knees. Slowly I reached out and touched his hands. They were like ice. Prising his fingers off the empty bottle I clasped one hand in mine.

'Mr Cheeseman,' I said gently.

Nothing. Not even a flicker.

I leaned towards him so that my lips were inches from his ear. A thick odour of alcohol and stale sweat and vomit filled my nostrils. Involuntarily my head recoiled and I gulped in some fresher air. Leaning in again I held my breath and spoke his name into his ear. There was no response. Releasing his hand I gripped his arm just below the shoulder. It was no thicker than a broomstick inside his jacket. I shook him gently.

'Mr Cheeseman?'

'Why are you whispering?' Arnold asked, peering down at me over his pile of blankets.

'I don't want to startle him.'

'Why not? Isn't that exactly what you want to do?'

I thought about this for a moment. Arnold had a point.

Turning my head for another lungful of fresh air, I squeezed the tramp's bony arm then leaned close to his ear and yelled his name as loud as I could.

'MR CHEESEMAN!!!'

As if he'd received a high-voltage electric shock, the old man sat bolt upright. His wide bloodshot eyes stared into mine and his awful, stale stench filled my nostrils. I had been so convinced poor Mr Cheeseman had already passed away that the sight of him sitting up was like seeing someone rise from the dead – like something from a zombie film. It scared me so much that I let out a terrified scream with my nose just inches from his. Hardly surprisingly Mr Cheeseman found the experience of being woken up and then screamed at pretty upsetting. So upsetting that he screamed back in my face, exactly as I had done but louder.

Recoiling from his rancid scream, I toppled back onto

my bum. This turned out to be a stroke of luck because Mr Cheeseman's natural reaction to being shouted at, shaken and screamed at was to defend himself. The punch he threw would probably have landed square on my nose if I hadn't fallen backwards.

For a moment we just stared at each other in wide-eyed silence. Both of our ribcages were going up and down like crazy as we fought for breath and tried to make sense of the last few seconds.

Hee-haw! Hee-haw! Hee-haw!

Mr Cheeseman and I both turned in the direction of the loud braying laughter. Arnold's head was back, his mouth wide open and his eyes tightly shut. He had let his pile of blankets and the plastic bag he was carrying fall to his feet. Both his arms were wrapped tightly around his ribcage.

Mr Cheeseman scratched his beard. 'D'you mind telling us what's so bloomin' funny, sunshine?' His speech was slow and slurred.

'I'm really sorry, Mr Cheeseman,' I said, glaring at Arnold. 'I didn't mean to startle you. We came to bring you some blankets and you were sleeping so soundly we weren't sure if...I mean, well, we wondered...you know...'

Mr Cheeseman shook his head. 'I haven't got a clue what you're going on about, Leon.'

'We thought you were dead,' Arnold said, his broad smile contrasting with his grim statement.

'Why on earth would you think that?' asked Mr Cheeseman.

'It's just that you were lying very still,' I said quickly. 'That's all.'

'And you're really old,' Arnold said helpfully. 'And incredibly thin – do you know you look just like a skeleton when you're sleeping? Plus there's the damage all that alcohol must be doing to your insides and living rough can't do your health any good at all so you probably haven't got long left anyway.'

'OK, I get it.' Mr Cheeseman laughed, holding up a hand in surrender. 'Although I should point out that I'm only fifty-one.'

Arnold's eyes ballooned with surprise. I knew what was coming next so I caught his eye and gave him a stern look to tell him to keep his mouth shut.

'Fifty-one!' Arnold exclaimed. 'I thought you were in your seventies at least. Why are you giving me that strange look by the way, Leon?'

'Never mind,' I mumbled.

'In my seventies? You cheeky ratbag.' Mr Cheeseman's wheezy laughter petered out and he looked at me. 'Do I really look like I'm in my seventies?'

My instinctive reaction was to assure him he looked

much younger than Arnold had guessed. That would have been easier than telling him the truth – for both of us. It would have been really awkward to confirm how old he really looked.

'Not at all,' I said.

Mr Cheeseman looked relieved but I wondered if I was letting him down by lying to him. Although Arnold had a distinctly tactless approach, maybe it was actually kinder to tell the truth sometimes – even if it wasn't good news. Perhaps if Mr Cheeseman knew how frail he'd become he might try and take better care of himself.

'Although,' I began tentatively, 'you do look older than fifty-one. Obviously a good spruce up would do you the world of good. But I'm sure you'd look, and feel, much younger and fitter if you stopped drinking? If you sobered up you could even get your life back on track – get a job. Maybe your wife would have you back?'

Mr Cheeseman harrumphed and shook his head.

'We could help you find her,' I suggested.

'I know where she lives,' Mr Cheeseman muttered bitterly. 'Sometimes I wait outside her house just to see her get into her car. The other day I got too close and she saw me. There wasn't the slightest flicker of recognition on her face. I was a total stranger to her. Just another tramp scavenging for food in the rubbish.'

'But if you stopped drinking and took better care of yourself?' Arnold wondered aloud.

'It's too late for that now,' Mr Cheeseman snarled. 'Far too much whiskey has flowed under the bridge – and into my stomach.'

'But we could help you,' I pleaded.

'I said NO.' Mr Cheeseman's face was pink with rage and wriggly veins stood out on his temples. 'Stop interfering in my affairs, will you? What gives you the right to tell me what to do? Why don't you sort out your own family before you start meddling with mine? How dare you lecture me on my drinking.'

I held Mr Cheeseman's wild stare. His milky blue irises were swimming on wide yellow eyeballs.

'Sorry,' I said quietly.

Mr Cheeseman exhaled and stared into his lap. Getting to my feet I picked up a few blankets and placed them next to the frail figure. 'We brought you these to keep you warm.'

He conveyed his gratitude with a single nod.

'And we got you dinner,' Arnold added. Next to the blankets he placed the plastic bag containing the sandwich and fizzy drink.

'Much obliged,' Mr Cheeseman mumbled into his chest.

I kneeled down and tidied the blankets Arnold had

dropped. 'Please give the blankets you don't want to any friends in need.'

Again Mr Cheeseman nodded. I stood, turned and walked away.

'Goodbye, Mr Cheeseman,' Arnold said before catching up with me.

'Well, that went well,' I muttered as we reached the high street. I clapped half-heartedly and gave my hands a brief shimmy.

'You did the right thing,' Arnold said.

'What? Made him really sad and angry?'

'Maybe he'll think about what you said. It might make a difference.'

'Maybe,' I said. But I wasn't so sure.

16

I was walking quickly, wondering if I'd done the right thing. Actually I was thinking I'd done completely the wrong thing. Had I really thought I could persuade Mr Cheeseman to change his lifestyle just by telling him how frail he looked? If he hadn't been able to stop drinking when his family depended on him, he was hardly likely to sober up just because some kid thinks he's not ageing well. All I'd achieved was reminding him how much he'd lost and insulting him at the same time. Talk about kicking a man when he's down.

The temperature was dropping fast as the sun dipped in the sky. Arnold had pulled his balaclava down to cover his face.

'You look ridiculous like that,' I said.

'I don't care what I look like,' he said proudly. 'My head is lovely and warm and I think you're just jealous.'

He had a point – my cheeks were freezing.

'Why are we hurrying anyway?' Arnold asked.

I just wanted to put as much distance between us and the mess I'd made of the conversation at the bus depot. 'I need to get home,' I said. 'I want to catch my sister before she sees Mum.'

I'd used seeing Olivia as an excuse for rushing because I didn't want to talk about Mr Cheeseman any more. But as soon as I mentioned her I started stressing about the broken window.

Arnold took out his mobile. 'I'm just going to ring the lady in the ticket office – see if there's any news.' He stopped walking and dialled.

I felt suddenly nervous about whether there'd be any tickets. I'd put it out of my mind for most of the day but now it was the moment of truth and my heart was racing. I couldn't bear to listen to Arnold's conversation in case it was bad news so I walked on about ten yards and stopped. I checked my phone. No message. I tried calling Olivia again but there was no answer, which was weird because she was permanently attached to her mobile. I tried a few more times but my sister didn't pick up.

Arnold was approaching, off the phone now.

I tried reading his expression to gauge how his phone call had gone but, as usual, it was blank.

'Well?' I said, my mouth dry.

'Fine, thanks,' he replied.

'What did she say? The lady in the ticket office.'

'Oh right.' Arnold frowned thoughtfully. 'She said, "Hello, Panthers ticket office. How may I help you?"'

I smiled patiently. 'OK. I guessed that part. I was more interested in how the conversation ended.'

'Well, why didn't you say that?' Arnold smiled amiably. 'It ended with her saying, "Goodbye now," and I said, "Bye bye."'

'I'm about this close to strangling you right now,' I muttered, holding up my thumb and forefinger about a centimetre apart.

Arnold looked perplexed. He said nothing.

With deliberate calmness, I asked, 'What did she say about the tickets for the match tomorrow?'

'Oh right. Well, it was quite confusing really. She said something about chickens and something about cards.'

I took a deep breath. 'Can you remember *exactly* what she said?'

Arnold thought carefully. 'She said, "I don't want to count my chickens, but think I may have come up trumps." I don't really know what that means.'

'You're a genius,' I laughed. 'It means she's confident she'll be able to get us some tickets.'

'Oh, OK. Well she told me to call her at ten-thirty tomorrow morning and she'll have a final answer.'

'I don't know how you do it, Arnold,' I said as we walked on together. 'But there's something about your direct approach that seems to get results.'

I felt elated and nervous at the idea we might actually get tickets for the match. What had seemed like a crazy plan now seemed to be nearly a reality. It looked like I would have to seriously put my mind to a problem I hadn't, up to this point, imagined facing. How was I going to organise my whole family to be in the same place at the same time?

'I just need to go in here,' Arnold said, coming to a standstill.

I stopped walking too and looked up at the building.

'What do you need to go in the bank for?' I asked.

'To get money,' Arnold replied. 'Isn't that what people usually go into banks for? We need it to buy the tickets.'

'Why don't you just use the ATM?'

Arnold shook his head. 'I haven't got my card on me. I need to speak to someone inside.'

He pushed open the bank's glass door and we went in. Two of the three teller windows were closed. About three metres away from the open window was a queue of about four people waiting patiently, while an elderly lady was counting the money she'd just withdrawn.

Arnold marched straight to the window, sidling round the elderly lady as she turned away from the counter, clipping her purse shut.

'Er – Arnold?' I whispered. 'I think all these people are queuing.'

Arnold turned and looked at the line of people. 'Sorry,' he said brightly, 'we won't be long.'

A couple tutted and a woman with a pushchair rolled her eyes. But nobody actually complained. Arnold stood in front of the window and leaned towards the bank clerk.

'Are you all right there?' the clerk asked in a monotone. She looked about the same age as the girls in year twelve. Her face was caked in orange make-up and false lashes framed her lifeless eyes.

'I'd like some money,' Arnold said. The effect of his balaclava was to make his request sound pretty menacing.

'I see.' There was faint tremor in the bank clerk's voice. 'I need to see your bank card and some identification please.'

Arnold shook his head. 'I don't have any ID. I just want some money.'

'I will need to see some ID, though.'

'I can tell you all my account numbers, my eight-digit passcode, my mother's maiden name and the name of my first pet if it helps.'

The clerk's smile was patronising. 'I am going to need to see some ID.'

'I haven't got any on me.'

'Please don't raise your voice at me.'

'I'm not raising my voice,' Arnold replied in what was, to be fair, quite a raised voice.

'Yes you are.'

'I am now – but I wasn't until you told me not to.'

At this point I decided to intervene. I leaned towards the teller's window to ask in a super calm and polite voice if there was any way at all that Arnold could withdraw money without ID – but the teller was gone.

'Where did she go?' I asked.

Arnold shrugged. 'She's just at the back, talking to that guy.'

I could see the bank clerk talking to an older man in a brown suit. 'He must be the bank manager,' I guessed. He looked very serious and they both kept glancing our way. Eventually the man in the brown suit started marching purposefully towards us. I was sure we'd be able to clear up any misunderstanding with the manager.

Arnold turned to the queue behind us and said, 'I'm very sorry about this. As soon as I've got the money I'll be on my way. There seems to be some sort of hold-up.'

The old man at the front of the queue looked startled. 'Did you say it's a hold-up?'

'Yes,' Arnold said impatiently. 'It's a hold-up.'

Everyone in the queue gasped. The young mum pulled her daughter close to her. One man at the back turned and scurried out the door.

'Did you say it's a *hold-up*?' asked the bank manager behind us.

Arnold turned and nodded at him. 'That's right. I'm holding up the bank so the sooner I get my money the better.'

I noticed the bank manager reach under the counter. I'd seen them do this in films – the plucky employee raising the alarm when they think the robbers aren't watching. In films the alarm sounds like a school bell and the employee gets shot for his bravery. That's what happened here too. I mean the sound of the alarm, not the manager getting shot.

'We've got to go,' I said, grabbing Arnold's arm.

'They won't give me my money,' he said, prodding a finger at the terrified bank manager on the other side of the glass.

'Never mind. Let's go.'

'I just want my money.'

'Listen,' I said as calmly as I could. 'I have a feeling the police are on their way. We need to go.'

'Why are the police coming?' Arnold's eyes gazed innocently through the two round holes in his balaclava.

I nodded at the bank manager. 'He's set off the alarm that tells the police someone's robbing the bank.'

Arnold's head turned sharply. 'Who's robbing the bank?' he whispered.

I smiled and whispered back, 'You are. Let's go.'

Before Arnold could ask any more questions, I yanked him by the arm, dragging him towards the door as fast as I could. Outside on the street I could hear the distant wail of a siren. I knew the sensible thing to do was to wait for the police and explain the misunderstanding to them.

In the split second I took to decide what to do I asked myself one simple question – what would Lenny have done?

'Run!' I yelled.

We sprinted down the high street and cut across the common and through the estate and over Chambers Park with Arnold's loose sole clapping us all the way. I heard another siren, closer than the first and imagined a police car closing in on us. (Looking back, it was more likely to have been responding to a domestic incident on the Blackwater estate or a snarl-up on the ring road. But I assumed it was chasing us so I put a burst of speed on.) I edged ahead of Arnold, laughing crazily.

As we approached the zebra crossing adjacent to Chambers Park I could see a bus approaching. I reached the kerb, stopped suddenly and pressed the button on the crossing.

But Arnold kept going.

Straight into the road.

'STOP!' I yelled.

A horn blared.

Arnold looked up, startled – and froze.

The bus was only doing about thirty but it was way too close to stop.

Horn blasting, the bus bore down on Arnold, about to swallow him up. Without thinking I ran into the road – in front of the bus – and threw myself at Arnold. Connecting with my shoulder I wrapped my arms round his waist, knocking him sideways. Together we hit the floor and sprawled across the road. The bus flashed past, inches from my face. Just a blur of colours and the smell of diesel. I felt its wake – hot air slapped my face and inflated my hood.

We clambered to our feet and stumbled to the opposite pavement then looked at each other, not speaking. My heart was racing. I watched the bus drive away. Somehow we had avoided disaster. For a few moments life had teetered on the brink of an abyss. But unlike a year ago it had not toppled tragically. Instead everything would carry on as normal.

'You OK?' I said.

Arnold nodded. 'Nice tackle.'

'That was close.'

'Yup.' He smiled. 'Thanks.'

We walked on together saying nothing.

After a while I said, 'I think you can take that off now.' I nodded at his head.

He grabbed the top of his balaclava and pulled it off. His face underneath was pink and shiny and his hair was a matted mess.

'I think we may have got away with it,' I said.

He nodded, smiling.

'In hindsight,' I said, 'it probably wasn't the smartest move to walk into a bank wearing a balaclava.'

'My head was cold,' Arnold protested. 'Is that why everyone thought I was trying to rob the place?'

'Partly,' I said. 'I think telling everyone it was a hold-up probably clinched it though.'

'But they were taking ages – oh wait...' Arnold stopped and rolled his eyes skyward for a moment. 'I didn't mean that kind of hold-up!'

'I can't believe you accidentally held up a bank,' I laughed. 'We'd better get you inside before you accidentally steal a car or something.'

'I'm too young to drive,' Arnold mumbled.

It felt good to have escaped from the police. It wasn't as if we'd committed a crime anyway – if we had, I think

171

I'd have felt far too guilty to run. It just seemed like the simplest solution to the misunderstanding. We'd avoided having to give a long explanation about the coincidental circumstances that made everyone think Arnold was trying to rob the bank. By doing so we'd saved the police a lot of wasted time questioning us so it felt like a success all round. Even though we hadn't really done anything wrong, getting away with it made me feel sort of … invincible.

17

Mum's car was in the drive so Arnold and I sneaked round to the side door. He waited outside while I went in to check if the coast was clear. Mum was in the living room and Olivia was in her room so I quickly ushered Arnold up the stairs.

'Can't I meet your mum now?' he asked.

I thought about this for about a nanosecond. I decided it would be better to assess the matter of the broken window before owning up to having a strange boy in the house. 'Maybe a bit later...' I replied, pushing him towards my bedroom. When Arnold was safely hidden away in my room I tiptoed up the landing and knocked on Olivia's bedroom door.

My sister was wearing a chunky cardigan, a scarf and a woolly hat. Sitting cross-legged on her bed she was sketching a dress design on a huge pad. She gave me a sympathetic smile as I entered and I knew immediately I was in trouble.

'Had an exciting day?' she asked.

For a moment I thought she was referring to the arcade and the bank job but when she held up my cricket ball I understood.

'Oh. Right. That. Does Mum know?'

'Of course she knows. She heard me scream when I came in and discovered the mess.'

'Oh, Livs,' I whined.

'What? I was shocked. I thought someone had broken in until I found the ball.'

'I left you a message on your phone,' I said. 'A couple of messages in fact. Didn't you get them?'

'Would that be on this phone?'

Olivia held up her mobile – a brand new satin silver iPhone. A brand new satin silver iPhone with a shattered screen.

'What happened to it?' I asked, but I already sort of knew I was responsible.

'I forgot to charge it last night,' Olivia explained. 'So I left it plugged in on my desk. Safe and sound – or so I thought.'

'Do you think the cricket ball smashed it?'

'Possibly,' Olivia made a confused face. 'Either that

or my phone was so sad about the broken window that it threw itself off the desk.'

I smiled guiltily. 'I'm really sorry, Livs.'

'Do you know how much these cost?'

'I'll pay you back.'

My sister's expression softened. 'Listen, don't sweat it.' Her smile was kind. 'I have to say, when I saw what you'd done I was about ready to pull out your fingernails one by one and soak your bleeding hands in hydrochloric acid.'

'Weirdly elaborate,' I mumbled.

'But I calmed down after a bit. Turns out I can claim on insurance so...'

'I'm off the hook?' I said with a hopeful smile.

'I wouldn't say *off* exactly. You still have Mum to contend with.'

'Oh shhhh...erbert. She's going to freak out, isn't she?'

'You bet I will.' It was Mum – standing so close behind me her voice buzzed in my ear.

I spun round. Smiled. Lenny used to be able to get away with murder with his smile. Judging by the expression on Mum's face, my winning smile needed work. But then I wasn't as practised as he had been. I hadn't used it to get out of trouble as much as Lenny.

'I'm sorry, Mum. It was an accident.'

'Cricket in the garden, Leon? What were you thinking?'

I shrugged and mumbled a 'Dunno'.

'Who were you playing with?'

'No one,' I said. 'It was only me. On my own. I was just knocking the ball up all alone and by myself.'

Mum nodded suspiciously. 'That ball could easily have ricocheted off a wall or the summer house and hit you on the head – you could have been killed.'

This scenario seemed unlikely but I knew better than to argue.

'No pocket money until you've paid for the broken window.'

I nodded solemnly.

'And the excess on your sister's insurance.'

More nodding.

'I'm really disappointed in you, Leon. With all that's happened to this family I could really do with you being more … responsible.'

'I said I'm sorry.'

'When Dad gets home I'll talk to him about a suitable punishment. For now I think it's best you go to your room. And you can stay there until I say otherwise.'

Mum turned and went downstairs.

'What does she mean *more responsible*?' I muttered.

'She doesn't mean anything,' Olivia replied. 'She just means she trusts you to behave.'

I shook my head. 'She means I should have learned my lesson after the damage I've already done to this family.'

'She doesn't mean that,' Olivia said.

'You don't see the way she looks at me.'

'You're imagining it.'

Before I could protest, Mum called Olivia downstairs to get her dinner. Mum would probably eat hers at her desk, Olivia on her lap in front of the TV. As my sister passed me in the doorway she ruffled my hair and whispered, 'Don't be so hard on yourself.'

I followed Olivia along the landing and watched her go downstairs. It was all right for her. She hadn't been at fault when Lenny was killed. I knew she missed Lenny as much as I did but she didn't have to live with the guilt or the blame. Soon she would finish college and she'd be out in the big wide world designing clothes and going to fashionable parties. I'd be stuck at home avoiding Mum because she blamed me for everything. Mum and Dad would continue to avoid each other, presumably because that was easier than facing the fact that the whole family was falling apart around them. Before long they'd split up and I'd see Dad every other weekend for some awkward activity where we both tried not to refer to Lenny in any way.

I went into my room expecting to see Arnold getting some much-needed practice on FIFA. But my room was empty.

I sneaked up the landing and knocked on the bathroom door. The door swung open a couple of inches and I peered inside. Empty.

Then I heard a sort of wooden clunk from Mum and Dad's room. As I approached I saw Arnold. He was standing next to my dad's bedside table just inside the doorway. In his hand was a shiny gold watch, which he was admiring in the light coming through the large sash window.

'Er, what are you doing?' I said calmly.

Arnold turned to face me. He didn't look embarrassed or surprised, he just smiled. 'This is a cool watch,' he said. 'How much did it cost?'

'Put it back.'

'I'm just looking at it. Must be worth thousands.'

'I said *put it back*.'

Without any sense of urgency Arnold placed the watch carefully back on the bedside table.

'What do you think you're doing in my parents' room?' I demanded.

'The door was open and I happened to notice the watch. I just stepped in to check it out. I really like watches – my dad used to have a nice watch.'

'Arnold.'

Arnold studied my face carefully. 'Wait, are you annoyed?'

'No, not at all. I'm absolutely fine with you snooping around my parents' bedroom.' I stepped towards Arnold, clapped and waved both hands in his face. He turned away and I felt immediately guilty for reacting aggressively.

'Look,' I said calmly. 'You can't just come in here and look at my dad's watch.'

'OK.' Arnold frowned. 'What else should I look at?'

'I mean you can't come in here, full stop.'

'Why not, question mark?'

I couldn't help smiling at Arnold's quizzical expression – the comical way he cocked his head to one side when he was confused.

I smiled briefly. 'We'd better go back to my room,' I said. 'In case someone sees you.'

Arnold followed me out of the room and I closed the bedroom door behind us. Safely hidden away in my room we turned on my Xbox. Sitting side by side we faced the screen waggling controls and tapping buttons with our thumbs.

'When am I going to meet your parents?' Arnold asked. 'I'd really like to meet them.'

Surprised, I turned to look at him but he just stared

at the TV. 'When the time is right,' I said. 'Soon. Probably not tonight, but soon.'

Later, I left Arnold playing Minecraft and crept downstairs to get some food. From halfway down the stairs I could see Mum and Olivia through the kitchen doorway. I sat down and watched them between the banisters, listening.

'I don't mind about the phone though,' Olivia said. 'It's all covered on insurance anyway.'

'I know, but that's not the point, Olivia.'

'What is then?'

'The point is that he was playing cricket in the garden for heaven's sake.'

'It's not like he robbed a bank or anything.'

'What's that supposed to mean?'

'Just that it's not exactly the worst thing he could have done.'

'He succeeded in smashing a window. Who knows what other damage he might have done – to the house or himself.'

'Is it really that dangerous?'

'What if he'd slipped on the grass and hit his head on the patio? Or knocked himself unconscious with the ball and fallen face-first into the pond?'

Olivia turned away from Mum to load a plate in the dishwasher and mumbled to herself, 'Not to mention being hit by a meteorite or struck by lightning.'

'What did you say?' Mum asked sharply.

Olivia turned and gave Mum a placating smile. 'It wouldn't hurt him to get into a bit of trouble every now and then.'

'What's that supposed to mean?'

'He's a teenage boy, Mum. They're supposed to get into trouble – that's what they do. Lenny was a little rascal – he used to get into trouble all the time.'

'And look what happened to him.' My mum's voice was brittle.

'Oh, Mum,' Olivia said softly. 'Lenny wasn't killed because he was a rascal. He was just in the wrong place at the wrong time. It was an accident.'

Mum said nothing for a moment. She plucked a tissue from the flowery box on the shelf and wiped her eyes. 'You're right,' she said quietly. 'But I'm Leon's mother and I'm going to do whatever it takes to make sure the same thing doesn't happen to him.'

'Whatever it takes?' Olivia said. 'Even if that means stifling every drop of his exuberance and enthusiasm?'

Mum was silent for a moment then her voice was hard. 'If that's what it takes, yes.'

Olivia left the kitchen and started climbing the stairs.

She didn't notice me sitting there until she was nearly on top of me.

'You scared me,' she smiled.

'Sorry,' I said. 'Thanks for sticking up for me.'

My sister shrugged. 'She'll chill out – one day.'

'Hope so. Listen – is there any chance you can do me a couple of massive favours. They're really important.'

'Before you ask, I'm not putting in a good word for you with Hannah.'

I feigned disappointment. 'Oh well – can you meet me in the Square tomorrow at two-thirty instead? It's really important.'

Olivia's eyes narrowed. 'What for?'

'You'll see.'

'Are you in some kind of trouble?'

'No – honestly. It's nothing like that. I've planned something – it's sort of a surprise. A nice surprise hopefully.'

'OK – I love surprises. I'll be there.'

'Great – thanks, Livs.'

'What was the other favour?'

I smiled sheepishly. 'Can you lend me forty quid?'

'Forty quid? What for?'

'For the surprise.'

'Listen, Leon,' Olivia sighed, 'I'm happy to stick up for you with Mum but I have to say you seem to be acting slightly strange at the moment. Sneaking around, breaking windows and now borrowing money. Are you sure you're OK?'

'I'm fine. I promise. I'm not involved in anything dodgy – I just need to borrow some money. Please, Livs.'

'You haven't got a secret Haribo habit, have you?' My sister placed a hand on my shoulder. 'I'll help you through it, but you have to want to give up.'

'Very funny. I'll pay you back – I promise.'

Olivia nodded earnestly. 'I'll think about it.'

18

After a late night playing Rainbow Six Siege on Xbox, Arnold and I woke at nine-thirty.

The house was quiet. I sneaked downstairs first and when I was sure we were alone I went back up for Arnold. We filled two bowls with Rice Krispies and, taking our breakfast into the lounge, we plonked ourselves down on the sofa and I switched on the TV.

'So where are we at?' I said, spooning cereal into my mouth.

'Er – in your house?' Arnold replied uncertainly.

'I mean about the tickets and everything. What time did you say you had to call that lady back?'

'She said ten-thirty.' Arnold checked his watch.

'Do you think she'll have them?' I asked. I was feeling agitated, talking quickly.

'I don't know.'

'But what do you *think*?'

'I *think* I don't know.'

'Did she say she'd *probably* come up trumps or she *might* come up trumps?'

'Yes.'

'Which one? Probably or might?'

'I can't remember.'

'How did she sound?'

'*A bit like this*,' said Arnold in a high-pitched, trembling voice.

'I mean, did she sound hopeful?'

'I don't know. Do a hopeful voice and I'll tell you if it sounds like her.'

'Uugh, we've got no chance have we?'

'Why not?'

'Well so far, you, me and Olivia are the only people who are definitely available for the match so I need to find a way of getting my parents to meet me to go to a game we haven't yet got tickets for and even if there are tickets available we haven't got enough money to pay for them.'

'There's always Mr Miller.'

'Who's he?'

'The man whose wallet we handed in. There might be a reward – you should ring Sergeant McIntosh and ask.'

'Yeah – and pigs might fly.'

I immediately felt bad about snapping at Arnold. And for deliberately using a metaphor to confuse him. I slumped back on the sofa and grabbed my phone, just for something to do. I noticed I had a text and a voicemail.

I dialled the voicemail number and listened. The message had been left earlier that morning when my phone was on silent. It was from a local landline.

'Good morning, Leon.' It was Sergeant McIntosh. She had that tone of voice people use when they're about to give some good news. Maybe Arnold had been right after all. 'Mr Miller came into the station to collect his wallet this morning and he was very grateful. Very grateful *indeed*.' This is it, I thought. Cash or tickets! Cash or tickets! 'He didn't offer any material reward but he did insist I pass on his immense gratitude…' I hung up. In a few days I might appreciate Mr Miller's gratitude but at that precise moment my needs were very much material. My mood had nosedived as I opened up my text message.

It was from Olivia. It said,

Hey Leon. I've put the money in the pocket of your Puffa.
Don't spend it all on Haribo. X

Suddenly my mood was lifted. Apart from the news that we actually had enough money to buy the tickets (if any were actually available) it occurred to me how fortunate I was to have a sister who looked out for me. Fortunate wasn't a feeling I'd had much of lately.

I went out to the hallway and delved into my Puffa pockets, returning to the lounge with two twenty-pound notes.

'Look at this,' I said brightly. 'Courtesy of my sister.'

Arnold grinned. 'What a cool sister.'

'Yup,' I said, sitting down again. 'I know.'

Picking up the Sky remote, I began flicking through the channels in search of something we would both enjoy. To be honest I had no idea what sort of TV show Arnold would like so I paused briefly on each channel to see if he would express any interest. It seemed that Arnold was just going to keep munching, whatever channel came on. So instead of waiting long enough for him to speak up I started playing this game with myself where I tried to see how quickly I could work out what the programme was about. On average I reckoned I could guess what was going on, on the basis of a two-second clip. In such a short snapshot I identified:

Sky news interviewing a politician about hospital waiting times

A cartoon about a team of animal superheroes

A programme about old people selling stuff they'd found in their attic

An American comedy about high school kids with magical powers

Something on the local news about a robbery at Lloyd's bank on Market Street

A show about people thinking of emigrating to Australia

SpongeBob SquarePants

Some sort of current affairs...WHOA!

Working my thumb as quickly as I could I flicked back to the local news report.

'Hey,' Arnold protested. 'I love SpongeBob.'

'Ssshhh!' I hissed, my eyes transfixed by the face on the screen. It was an egg-shaped face sprouting thick black whiskers with a black smear on each cheek.

'Yeah, they came into my shop yesterday,' said the man on the TV, his beady eyes darting between the camera and the interviewer. *'There was two of them – one average, the other tall and solid. They were just kids. Barely teen-agers. They bought a whole bunch of blankets and a balaclava. Probably the one they were wearing when they did the bank job.'*

'Hey,' Arnold yelped, dribbling milk and soggy Rice Krispies into his lap. 'That looks just like the guy from the army surplus store.'

'That's because it *is* the guy from the army surplus store.'

188

'What's he—?'

'Just listen.'

The TV reporter asked, *'Did the two suspects say they were planning to hold up a bank?'*

The man shook his egghead. *'I could just tell. When you've got as much experience as I have in combat situations you pick up a sort of sixth sense. You can smell an insurgent a mile away.'*

'I see.' The reporter nodded wisely. *'And have you seen active service yourself?'*

The shop assistant looked into the camera, then at the reporter and back to the camera. He rolled his chin as if his collar was suddenly too tight. Then, with an almost imperceptible shake of his head, he said, *'Not in the actual army, no. But I have got a Purple Heart on Call of Duty.'*

The news report cut to a shot of the journalist standing outside the bank.

'It was at this small branch of Lloyd's bank on Market Street that the attempted robbery took place yesterday after-noon at approximately 4.32 p.m. Two individuals, believed to be male youths, entered the bank through the main door. The one wearing a black balaclava to protect his identity proceeded to the teller's window where he demanded money. When the brave teller – young Amy Whitlock – refused, the suspect grew agitated. When Amy went to inform her

189

manager, the suspect announced that he was holding up the bank. This CCTV footage shows the terrifying moment a handful of innocent bystanders were caught in the middle of the attempted robbery.'

The grainy black-and-white film was taken from a camera that must have been mounted above the entrance to the bank. It showed Arnold and me marching past the queue and straight up to the teller window. When Arnold turned to address the queue the young mum clutched her child towards her and a man at the back scurried to the door.

The report cut back to the journalist. 'Shortly before attempting to rob the bank, the two suspects were spotted distributing blankets to homeless people at the bus depot. One homeless man who received some blankets yesterday identified himself as Mr Cheeseman but couldn't confirm the identity of the mystery pair. When I spoke to him he would only say that he had received the blankets from people he considered "dear friends".'

I felt a strange surge of emotion hearing that Mr Cheeseman had described us as friends. I hadn't realised how anxious I'd been about the cross words we'd exchanged at the bus depot.

The reporter continued, 'Police believe the two suspects may have paid for the blankets with the proceeds of an earlier crime, although none has so far been reported.'

The reporter turned to Detective Inspector Woolly. '*It is mere speculation*,' said a nervous-looking police officer, '*but, at this present moment in time, we are working on the possibility that the pair are embarking on a Robin Hood crime spree to protest about social injustice and raise awareness about the plight of homeless people.*'

'Did you hear that?' I said, as the reporter handed back to the studio. 'We're the Robin Hood Robbers.'

'Cool,' Arnold grinned.

'What do you think we should do?'

He looked at me and shrugged. 'Xbox?'

'I mean about being the Robin Hood Robbers.'

'What? Like should we rob from the rich and give to the poor?'

'No,' I said, feeling myself getting stressed. 'I mean should we hand ourselves in?'

'But we haven't done anything,' he said. 'There was no robbery and we bought those blankets ourselves out of our winnings.'

'Winnings we got from underage gambling on a fruit machine.'

'It's not like we stole the Crown Jewels or anything though...'

Reluctantly I let myself be persuaded by Arnold's logic. We hadn't actually committed any crime so there was nothing to feel guilty about. Instead of worrying any more about whether we were doing the right thing or not I decided to get a glass of apple juice.

As I entered the kitchen I noticed someone had left the fridge door open. I didn't think I'd done it. I'm normally pretty good at shutting it because Mum goes off on one if I leave it open for even a moment while I think about what I fancy. For her any visit to the fridge has to be like an SAS raid – in, out, job done. Dad was the only one who ever stood at the fridge with the door open and he was always getting it from Mum for doing it.

Anyway I was just about to push the fridge door to when it shut by itself. Well, that's what it looked like except as it closed I saw Dad standing behind it.

'Whoa, you scared me,' I said, laughing. Already I was wondering how to keep him out of the lounge.

'Who did you think I was, the fridge burglar?' My dad looked tired, but he was freshly spruced as usual – wearing a polo shirt and chinos. He smiled brightly and wiped his mouth with the back of his hand.

'No,' I shook my head gravely. 'But I am going to have to arrest you though for loitering in front of an open fridge and drinking from a family-sized juice carton.'

'Guilty as charged.' He held up his hands. 'Don't tell Mum – she'll have me breaking rocks in a Siberian gulag.'

'OK, I'll let it go just this once.' I wagged my finger. 'But don't let me catch you breaking the law again.'

'Thank you, officer.'

'Have you spoken to Mum?' I asked, remembering her promise to tell Dad about the broken window.

'What about?' Dad asked, his eyes narrowing.

'Nothing in particular,' I said innocently.

Dad shook his head. 'I got home late last night and your mum left before I woke this morning. I think she's out doing her road safety thing.'

'What are you up to today?'

'I'm playing golf with some clients.' He checked his watch – a chunky black one with orange numbers. 'I'd better get a move on. I don't want to miss my tee-off time.'

I watched him walk to the utility room where he sat on the bench to put on his shoes.

'What time will you be finished?' I asked.

Dad glanced at his watch again. 'About three I guess. Why?'

I felt my heart sink. 'Oh – no reason. I was really hoping we could do something later.'

'Such as?'

I didn't want to mention the rugby. It was something we always did with Lenny and I didn't want to scare off my dad. It would be much better to break it to everyone later – when we were all together. I shrugged. 'Dunno really.'

'OK – well, when I get home maybe we can do something then. How's that?'

I smiled.

Picking up his golf shoes, my dad opened the door and paused, turning back.

'What did you get up to yesterday?'

'Nothing.' Too defensive. 'I mean, nothing in particular.'

'As long as you didn't get into any mischief?'

'Oh, you know me. Just a handful of misdemeanours and the odd felony.'

'That's my boy.'

When he closed the door I felt a deep sense of longing. I yearned for the time Lenny, Dad and I used to spend together. I missed the easy conversations we used to have. It would be so cool to be able to talk to him without worrying that we might end up talking about Lenny.

'Who were you talking to?' Arnold asked from the lounge.

'Dad. He's gone to play golf – he won't be back in time for the rugby.' I sat down with a sigh. 'I guess that scuppers our plan to watch the match later.'

'Not necessarily,' said Arnold with a devious smile. 'Which golf club does he belong to?'

'The Park, why?'

Arnold tapped on his phone for a few moments then held it to his ear. 'Oh good morning,' he said at last, putting on a gruff voice. 'Is that The Park Golf Club? It's Mr Copeman speaking. I'm really sorry but I'm going have to cancel my tee-off time today...'

'I can't believe you did that!' I said when Arnold came off the phone.

'I'd never given a false name before we met, now I can't stop myself,' he laughed. Then, glancing at his watch, he said, 'It's ten-thirty. I'd better call the ticket office.'

I felt suddenly sick with nerves. I couldn't stand to watch Arnold make the call so I took our bowls out to the kitchen. When he'd finished I went back into the lounge, dreading the outcome of his conversation.

'Have they got the tickets?' I said, eagerly.

'Sold out,' he said, shaking his head gravely.

'No way.' I dropped onto the sofa. I knew it was just a rugby game and we'd only hatched the plan to go the day before. But it had become more important than that. It was a chance to remember Lenny. And it was a chance for a fresh start.

I felt drained.

Then Arnold clapped and did jazz hands and burst out laughing and I realised he'd been winding me up and I laughed too.

'So we have got tickets then?'

Arnold couldn't answer me for ages because he was

braying so hard. For a while this was pretty funny but then I just wanted a straight answer and he was still laughing.

'I'm getting annoyed now,' I said sternly. 'Have we got tickets or not?'

Arnold wiped a tear from his plump cheek and nodded. 'We just need to pick them up later,' he wheezed. 'The lady I spoke to normally works in the hospitality suite on match days but she'll meet us in the club shop at two o'clock.'

'That's amazing,' I said. 'We can collect the tickets at two then meet my family in the Square at half past. I've already arranged to meet my sister and now my dad's going to be available so I can call him later and ask him to meet me there. All I have to do now is find a way of getting my mum there.'

I felt strangely excited about the prospect of getting everyone together to watch the match. To remember Lenny and the amazing day we had at the match last year. To acknowledge how much we missed him – but also to begin again as a family. Just the four of us.

19

It was pretty sunny and we had some time to kill so Arnold and I decided to head down to the beach. I lent him my bike and I took Lenny's old one. He cycled like a madman, weaving round pedestrians on the pavement and swerving on and off the road. I rode along steadily, shouting at Arnold to be careful. It seemed like the more I told him to watch out, the more crazy he got so in the end I shut up and let him get on with it.

I followed Arnold down to the pier, then I sped ahead of him when we were away from the roads, along the cliff top for a few miles. At last I slowed down and came to a stop, sweating and panting. Arnold yanked on his brakes and his back wheel jerked sideways, skittering tiny stones across the Tarmac path.

'What are we doing?' he asked.

'Going down there.' I nodded to the small rocky cove

about thirty metres below us. A narrow crescent of yellow sand was squeezed between the crystal blue sea and the rusty cliff face. 'Lenny and I used to come here and pretend we were smugglers. There's a wicked cave in the rocks.'

As I spoke I felt my voice wobble. I realised I hadn't been to 'Smugglers' Cove' (as we used to call it) since Lenny died. We'd always treated it as our own secret beach but something had made me want to share it with Arnold that morning.

'Great.' Arnold grinned and let my bike fall into a gorse bush. Maybe that was why I'd wanted to bring him. Anyone else I knew would have been all *sensitive* about Lenny's memory – tiptoeing respectfully around my feelings. But I was tired of feeling sad every time I remembered my brother.

As I rested Lenny's bike on top of mine, my mobile rang. It was my mum.

'Leon? Is everything all right?'

'Hi, Mum. Yeah everything's fine.'

'Where are you?'

'Just out on my bike.'

'Not on the roads?'

'No, Mum – on the pavement.'

'I hope you're being careful crossing roads.'

'I always am.'

'Where are you going?'

'Nowhere really.'

There was a pause then my mum said, 'Are you wearing your helmet?'

'Of course.'

'What time will you be home?'

I glanced at my watch. 'In a couple of hours or so.'

'I'm not sure you should—'

'Mum,' I said sternly. 'I'm not a baby. I'll look after myself.'

'I'll call you in a while.'

'OK. Mum?'

'Yes?'

'Can you do me a really big favour?'

'What is it?'

'Can you meet me in the Square at two-thirty?'

'What for?'

'Can you?' There was silence on the line. My heart was willing my mum to understand – to sense how important this was for me.

'I can't, Leon. I have a meeting with Councillor Thomas at two-thirty. I want to talk to him about lowering the speed limit outside St John's school.'

'It's really important, Mum.'

'More important than the safety and wellbeing of three hundred primary school kids?'

I breathed out and shook my head wearily. 'Never mind. See you later then.'

I slipped my phone into my pocket, unclipped my helmet and hung it on the handlebars of Lenny's bike. I could feel my eyes filling up. Anger and frustration welled up inside me and I sprinted past Arnold towards the zigzag pathway worn down the steep slope. 'Race you to the bottom!' I called over my shoulder.

'Wait!' I heard Arnold cry as I hurdled a stray bramble. I didn't stop to explain and he chased me down the slope. I could tell he was gaining on me by his panting breath and flapping shoe getting louder. As I slowed to go round each hairpin bend in the path I felt him close in on me so that he was almost within touching distance.

The last fifty metres was a straight line down a steep bank onto the sand. Arnold and I sprinted down the final stretch for all we were worth, first me then him edging slightly ahead. As we reached the beach we both collapsed onto the soft sand, laughing and breathlessly claiming victory.

'I won,' Arnold laughed.

'No way.' I'd got rid of some of my frustration. 'I won. But I think you're getting faster.'

We argued for a little while longer then fell silent and stared up at the wide blue sky, our chests heaving. The air smelled of salt and seaweed. I thought of holidays by the sea. Ice cream and sandcastles and Lenny and me in matching trunks.

After a while Arnold turned his head to look at me. 'Did you always come here with Lenny?'

I turned to meet his gaze. Nodded.

'Did you two do everything together?'

I nodded again. 'We went to school together every day. We had the same lessons together and we played together at lunchtime. We spent our weekends together and we did all the same clubs. Even played in the school rugby team together.'

'You must miss him a lot.'

I felt a lump grow in my throat and I swallowed hard. 'Yup.' I tried to smile. 'A lot.' I thought about stuff for a while then said, 'I think I miss him even more because now I'm not allowed to do any of the things we used to do together.'

'Like rugby?'

'Rugby, football, you name it.'

'What about tennis?'

'Are you kidding? According to my mum a whack on the head from a tennis ball could easily kill me.'

'So what can you play – tiddlywinks?'

'Now you're just talking crazy!' I laughed. 'One of those flying counters could have my eye out. Not to mention the potential choking hazard.' I clapped and did apathetic jazz hands to show I was joking. But only just.

Arnold sighed heavily. 'Must be weird – missing your brother and missing out on playing with your mates. You must feel lonely.'

His last word touched something inside me and I turned my face away from his, blinking. I felt a tear spill out of the corner of my eye and roll back, down the side of my head into my ear.

'You're crying.'

'I'm not.'

'It's OK to cry. My mum never does. If she did then I might have known how sad she was. I don't know why people always hide how they feel – pretending they're happy when they're not, or pretending something's not funny when it is. Life would be much simpler if everyone cried when they are sad, screamed when they are angry and laughed when they are happy.'

'Like you do,' I said, turning to face Arnold again.

He nodded. 'I can't help saying what's on my mind. I know people think I'm weird, but I can't help it. I can tell people are thinking, "This is a bit awkward, Arnold" but I don't have that mental filter most people have. If something pops into my mind it comes out of my mouth a second later.'

'I like your honesty. I mean it was a bit of a shock at

first but now I'm used to it, it's cool. It must get you into trouble sometimes though?'

'Teachers and other grown-ups are always telling me I have *behavioural problems* just because I say what I think. There is always someone trying to label me with this syndrome or that disorder. Mum is only one who understands me. She just used to tell me never to change – that she loved me just as I was.'

'I envy you,' I said. 'There's a lot of things I wish I could say.'

'Just say them. What's the worst that can happen?'

I thought about that for a moment. Maybe Arnold was right.

'So where's this cave then?' Arnold asked.

I nodded at the low headland protruding from the rocky cliff at the far end of the moon-shaped beach. 'Just round those rocks. It's quite a low entrance but it opens out into a massive cavern. You have to be careful though – when the tide starts to come in it cuts the cave off in a jiffy.'

'Why do you call it Smugglers' Cove?'

I smiled. 'Lenny and I used to play pirates in there. One time he discovered some smooth pebbles at the back of the cave. They're hidden away under a low overhang of rock, like a cluster of bronze and gold ingots.'

'So you pretended they were hidden treasure?'

'You say that like it's really lame,' I said defensively.

Arnold shrugged. 'I haven't played pirates since I was about seven, that's all.'

'Yeah, well maybe if you'd had a twin brother you would have done.'

Arnold frowned and shook his head. 'I don't think so.'

Annoyed by Arnold's reaction, I flopped back on the sand and closed my eyes. I used to do this when Lenny and I had disagreed. I don't mean I always flopped back onto the sand because there wasn't always sand around when we disagreed. I mean I used to sulk. Eventually Lenny would come over and try and cheer me up – make silly faces or come up with a stupid game to play. I thought of him suggesting we play chase the morning he was killed and a feeling of utter despair washed over me. If only I hadn't been in such a grumpy mood that day.

The thing about grief was that I never knew when it was going to strike. Most of the time it just left a black cloud over everything so that even the brightest day felt wintry. But sometimes, often without warning, the sadness would grab me, squeezing me so tight I could hardly breathe and wringing every drop of energy out of me.

That's what happened when I thought about Lenny trying to cheer me up on the way to school just before the accident. Lying on the sand, I felt suddenly exhausted.

I felt my cheeks glowing in the hot sun and my mind drifted lazily.

'My mum can't come to the match,' I announced at last.

'Why not?'

I sat up and combed a hand through the sand. 'She's meeting some councillor dude to talk about road safety.'

Arnold's eyes lit up. 'I could call pretending to be the councillor and cancel their meeting. Like I did with your dad's golf?'

I thought about this then shook my head. 'That won't work for a couple of reasons. Firstly I think she has this guy's number in her phone so your mobile number will look suspicious. And secondly he's got this really raspy cockney voice – like some old alchie that smokes forty a day. I met him once when he came round our house.'

'Oh right,' Arnold replied. 'So we need to persuade someone else to call your mum. Some old cockney with a hoarse voice and preferably their own landline. Who could we ask?'

I felt a big smile spread across my face. 'I've got it!' I said.

'Me too!' Arnold clapped.

'Are you thinking who I'm thinking?'

'Yup.' Arnold grinned and nodded. 'Jason Statham.'

'Jason Statham the Hollywood actor?'

'Uh-huh. He's cockney, isn't he?'

'Sure,' I said and Arnold beamed proudly. I continued, 'I'm just not sure we'll be able to get in touch with a world-famous film star and persuade him to ring my mum and pretend to be Councillor Thomas.'

'Good point.' Arnold grimaced. 'Who were you thinking of?'

I smiled. 'Mr Cheeseman.'

20

'Oh, hello,' said Mr Cheeseman – his voice sounding even more croaky than normal. 'Is that Mrs Copeman? It's Councillor Thomas speaking.'

Mr Cheeseman was standing under the canopy of the payphone next to the bus depot. He was clutching the big plastic receiver to his ear and studying his feet, head bowed.

It had taken us a while to persuade him to make the call. His main objection was that it was an offence to impersonate a town councillor. Nor was he comfortable with the idea of lying to my mum – especially as she had been so kind in preparing her chicken fricassee for him. As usual, I hadn't corrected him on what he'd actually had to eat but his addled memory was a real worry. Instead I had pleaded with him to make the phone call.

'I'm just not sure I'm comfortable with pulling the wool over your old dear's eyes like that,' he had said, shaking his head.

'There won't be any wool,' Arnold had insisted, unnecessarily. 'Please, Mr Cheeseman. It's just a quick phone call. Leon's trying to get his family together. His parents hardly ever see each other and when they do they barely speak. They never spend any time as a family – it's like they're all avoiding any mention of the fact that Lenny's gone.'

'Is that so?' Mr Cheeseman had asked me.

I'd nodded. 'Nobody mentions him. I want to talk about him but I don't want to upset everyone else by bringing up his name. The only thing is we're all trying so hard not to talk about Lenny that we don't talk about anything. Mum and Dad seem more distant than ever and Olivia's leaving home soon. If I don't do something now, I'm scared the whole family will fall apart. Arnold has managed to blag some tickets for the rugby match today. Lenny loved rugby and I want us all to go to the match. To remember him – and to start spending time together again.'

'Well, we can't risk your family going through any more heartache, can we, sonny?' Mr Cheeseman had winked a rheumy eye. 'Come on then – let's have your mum's number. We haven't got all day.'

Arnold and I watched Mr Cheeseman in silence, trying to gauge from his expression whether my mum believed he was Councillor Thomas.

'Do I?' he said, turning and pulling a face at us. 'Well, I've got this terrible cold at the moment. It's been a right pain.'

Cupping his hand over the mouthpiece, he whispered to me, 'She says I sound much more croaky than normal.' Then he continued, into the phone. 'What's that?' Glaring at me he started talking in an exaggerated Welsh accent. 'Well, you see, my Welshness comes and goes – isn't it? I've been spending a lot of time in London recently so I suppose I may have picked up some estuary English along the way.'

Mr Cheeseman listened, nodding.

'Well, this is it. I mustn't let my Welsh accent diminish too much or people will start to think I'm a fraud!' He laughed nervously. 'Anyway, the reason for my call is that I was wondering if we might change the venue of our meeting later? If possible I was hoping you would meet me in the Square this afternoon – at two-thirty? ... I shall look forward to it as well. There's lovely. Bye for now.'

Mr Cheeseman hung up with a sigh. 'It's a good job I've got some experience of working undercover, I can tell you that for nothing.'

'Did she believe you?' Arnold asked.

'I think so,' Mr Cheeseman nodded. 'Although, for the record, it turns out Councillor Thomas isn't a gruff Londoner at all but softly spoken. And from Wales.'

'That's weird,' I said. 'I'm sure he came round our house once and was really gruff and...oh hang on.' I felt a pulse go through me. 'Come to think of it that was Councillor *Thompson*. Sorry.'

Mr Cheeseman laughed. 'I think you'd better reconsider any plans you had to join the intelligence services.'

'I think you're right,' I said sheepishly. 'Thank you for doing this, Mr Cheeseman. It means a lot.'

'Don't mention it. I hope it helps keep your family together. Family matters more than anything. I know that better than anyone.'

Mr Cheeseman smiled but his eyes were sad. I smiled back.

'See you soon, Mr Cheeseman,' said Arnold and we both turned to leave.

'By the way,' Mr Cheeseman said. 'I hope you two had nothing to do with that incident at the bank yesterday?'

'Ah,' I said, 'that was just a misunderstanding.'

'I wasn't trying to rob the place,' said Arnold. 'I just accidentally told them it was a hold-up.'

Mr Cheeseman let out a wheezy laugh. 'Well, it might be worth you two stopping by the station some time to explain.'

I considered his idea for a moment and realised he was right. 'We will,' I promised. 'Tomorrow.'

21

On the way home I got a text from my dad. He said there'd been a mix-up with his golf so he was free this afternoon after all. I sent a message back asking if he could meet me in the Square at two-thirty and he sent back a thumbs-up emoji. I couldn't believe it. I was actually going to get everyone together at the same time for the big match. I hoped they would all understand that I wanted to talk about Lenny and remember him. I felt slightly sick with nerves.

When we got home Arnold wanted some toast. There was a fresh loaf in the bread bin. I got the jam and butter out of the fridge and handed him a small butter knife.

'Help yourself,' I said. 'I'm just going to change. We'll head out to the stadium in about half an hour.'

I went to my room and opened my chest of drawers. My Panthers rugby shirt was folded at the bottom of a pile of tops – where it had remained untouched for the last year. As I unfolded it I had this weird feeling of déjà vu. I saw myself, full of excitement, unfolding the same shirt to wear to last year's match. It was a memory so powerful it was like it was actually happening. For a moment I expected Lenny to come bounding into the room in his Panthers shirt singing a rude song about thrashing the Kestrels.

As I buttoned the collar (Owen Ritchie always wears his rugby shirt buttoned up) I noticed my phone lying on my desk. The previous day I'd been telling Arnold about the song 'He Ain't Heavy, He's My Brother', by The Hollies, because it always makes me think about Lenny. He'd never heard it so I'd promised to play it to him but in the excitement of winning big on the fruit machine, acciden- tally holding up a bank and almost getting hit by a bus, I'd forgotten about it.

I slipped my Beats headphones on and scrolled through the tunes. I knew the song was on an old playlist, I just wasn't sure which one. As I searched for it, I stum- bled upon other tunes I'd completely forgotten about that Lenny and I used to sing along to. I ended up lying on my bed, listening and reminiscing. I didn't know how long I spent there, cocooned in my own little world – absorbed in tunes and lyrics and soaking in the memories they conjured up.

It had slipped my mind that the reason I'd started listening to music in the first place was to find 'He Ain't Heavy' for Arnold. When another song ended and the sound of The Hollies filled my head I jumped off the bed with a start.

Arnold! I'd forgotten all about him.

With my headphones still on at the top of the stairs I was blissfully ignorant of the dramatic scene I was about to enter. On the landing, the faint whiff of burnt toast filled my nostrils and it occurred to me I should have shown Arnold how to adjust the settings on the toaster.

I checked my watch. One-thirty. Time to go to the stadium to pick up the tickets. I jogged down the stairs eagerly. The whole crazy plan seemed to be coming together.

I was about halfway down when I noticed the front door was open. I was curious but not anxious. Maybe Arnold had popped outside for some reason – chucking some burnt toast in the dustbin perhaps? A few more steps down I noticed a policeman's navy trousers and his shiny black boots.

In a split second I knew my plan was about to be derailed. It was like all the guilt and regret that I'd ignored over the past few days hit me in one go. As if it had been stored up inside me, just waiting for the time to explode.

I slipped off my headphones and watched the scene

play out in the kitchen. Olivia was wielding a loaf of French bread like a baseball bat. Arnold was armed with a butter knife and a slice of toast, while the police constable tried to persuade them both to step away from their bakery items. I wondered whether it was even worth mentioning that I had just been about to own up about having Arnold to stay. I felt like lying about bringing him home was worse than being wanted for the bank job. The things I felt guilty about, in descending order of regret were:

1. Bringing Arnold home without telling my family.
2. Not owning up to having Arnold in the house.
3. Asking Olivia to cover for me breaking her window.
4. Getting annoyed with Olivia for not covering for me when the reason she hadn't was because I'd smashed her mobile phone (as well as her window).
5. Accidentally holding up a bank.
6. Not owning up to accidentally trying to rob a bank.
7. Playing cricket in the garden.

The police officer finally convinced Olivia to put down the French bread then Arnold laid his butter knife on the counter. At that point I was still thinking I might be able to talk my way out of it. But when Arnold called me by name the game was up.

214

When the policeman asked me to confirm where I'd been the previous afternoon at the time of the attempted bank robbery, I tried to buy some time by telling them it was a funny story.

'If I wanted to hear a funny story I'd have asked you if you have any funny stories,' he said, with a surprising amount of authority. 'I want you to confirm your whereabouts yesterday afternoon between 4.32 and 4.44 p.m.'

I considered my options. Glanced at Arnold. Swallowed. After another moment of excruciating silence, Arnold and I both spoke at once. Incredibly we both came up with a really convincing alibi at the exact same moment.

Predictably though, the alibis we gave were different. I said we'd been messing around on the beach and Arnold said we'd been in Chambers Park.

'I think you two had better accompany me to the station, don't you?' said the officer.

I thought about the lady waiting to meet us in the gift shop at the stadium with the match tickets.

'But we have to be somewhere at two,' I said desperately.

The police officer snorted. 'I shouldn't think so, sunshine.'

As Arnold and I traipsed out of the house, shadowed by the policeman, Olivia followed.

'You can't come,' I said.

'You're joking,' she said with a smile so kind I wanted to hug her (but I didn't in case the policeman thought I was trying to pass her incriminating evidence or something). 'I'm not letting you go on your own. I'll call Mum and Dad and get them to meet us at the station – they'll sort this out.'

'You can't tell them,' I urged. 'You have to go to the Square at two-thirty. Mum and Dad will be there. You have to keep them there until I arrive.'

'I can't let you go to the station on your own...'

'Please, Liv. It's really important. I've got us all tickets to the rugby match this afternoon. I want us all to do something together – to remember Lenny, but also to try and start again.'

'I take it Mum and Dad don't know?'

I shook my head. 'Promise me you won't tell them?'

She nodded.

'And promise me you'll be in the Square at half-two?'

My sister looked dubious.

'Promise me, Liv.'

'OK,' she said with an encouraging smile. 'See you at two-thirty.'

Arnold and I were sitting on metal chairs in a small windowless room at the back of the police station. The police officer from the kitchen was standing the other side of a battered desk. Nobody spoke. The hands of the clock on the wall crawled round. When they reached two o'clock I couldn't contain my frustration any longer.

'What are we waiting for?' I asked, quickly adding, 'Sir?' to make up for my tone.

The constable sighed. 'We are waiting for the Duty Station Sergeant to question you regarding the attempted robbery of Lloyds Bank on Saturday afternoon.'

'We can explain,' I said.

'You'd better hope you can.'

'You'll laugh when you hear what happened, won't he, Arnold?'

Arnold studied the police officer carefully. 'It's really hard to say ... Maybe.'

'I'm not in a laughing mood.'

Arnold pulled a face. 'In that case, maybe not.'

'You see,' I continued, as if I'd been encouraged to tell my story, 'we went into the bank to withdraw some money but there was a delay because Arnold didn't have his bank card on him. When he explained to the queue behind us that there was a hold-up he just meant 'hold-up' as in a delay but of course they thought he meant 'hold-up' as in a robbery. It was probably something to do with the fact that Arnold was wearing a balaclava at the time. Next thing we knew the manager had set off the alarm thinking we were trying to rob the place! It really was quite comical.' I'd been grinning inanely as I spoke in an attempt to entice the police officer into seeing the funny side.

His face remained completely deadpan. 'That's quite a story,' he said. 'I'm sure the Duty Station Sergeant will enjoy hearing it.'

I didn't quite know how to take that. I glanced anxiously at the clock. 'How much longer do you think this will take?'

'How long is a piece of string?'

'What string?' asked Arnold.

Nobody replied.

Time ticked by.

At twenty past two the door opened and another policeman stepped into the room. There was short whispered conversation between the two officers before the visitor left.

'OK, boys,' our guardian announced sharply. 'On your feet.'

'Where are we going?' I asked. A tiny chink of hope made me think he might be letting us go.

'I have to take you to interview room six. Follow me.'

Arnold and I got up and shuffled out of the room while

the constable marched proudly ahead of us. He led us past the station desk and down a long corridor with lots of doors leading off it.

'Are we going to speak to the sergeant now?' I asked. That glimmer of hope allowed me to believe we might still make it to meet my family and that the lady in the rugby club shop may have saved our tickets for us.

The policeman stopped outside a door with a plastic number six screwed to it.

'Is this interview room six?' asked Arnold.

'How did you work that out, Einstein?' sneered the constable.

'Because of the number on the door,' Arnold said. 'And by the way, my name isn't Einstein.'

The policeman opened the door and indicated we should go in with a jerk of his head. Inside the room, on the far wall, a clock said it was nearly twenty-five to three. I felt my heart sink. I pictured my family in the Square, stranded amidst the sea of rugby supporters heading to the game. I felt this overwhelming urge to be with them. If I didn't get there they would be swamped and lost in the crowds – swept away and separated for ever. But I knew there was no hope. It was too late.

As I stepped into the interview room I heard a door open behind me. Instinctively I turned and found myself looking at the square-jawed, heavy-browed face of Sergeant McIntosh. I realised she must be the Duty Station Sergeant we were waiting to talk to and I felt a glimmer of hope inside my belly.

'Well, well, look who it is!' she exclaimed warmly. 'My favourite two do-gooders. Although you're cutting it a bit fine, aren't you?'

'Cutting what fine?' asked Arnold.

'The time,' the sergeant laughed. 'I was beginning to think you didn't get my message.' She looked at us both for a moment, decoding the expressions on our faces. 'Wait. You *didn't* get my message, did you?'

I felt like I did at school when I hadn't been listening properly to what Mr Beaston was saying about trigonometry. 'I got the part about there being no reward from the guy whose wallet we handed in,' I said.

'What about the other part?' Sergeant McIntosh enquired, folding her fleshy arms.

I shook my head. I could feel my face going red. 'I didn't listen to the rest of it,' I confessed. 'I sort of got distracted...'

'Distracted, were you?' Sergeant McIntosh huffed. 'Well, if you didn't get my message asking you to meet me here at two-fifteen then what is it that brings you here?'

'I apprehended them myself,' the policeman from my kitchen announced, with a smug grin. 'These two individuals are here for questioning in relation to the attempted robbery of Lloyds Bank at approximately 4.32 p.m. in the afternoon, yesterday...afternoon.'

Sergeant McIntosh's straight mouth curved into a broad grin. 'Are you serious?' she laughed.

The policeman nodded solemnly. 'I have already obtained a partial confession but it was not during an official interview. According to protocol I am escorting them to interview room six where we will wait for you to conduct a formal cross-examination when you have completed the duty with which you are presently engaged upon.'

'Honestly, Constable Saunders, I do wish you would speak in plain English sometimes.'

'Yes, ma'am.'

'Tell me about this confession.'

Constable Saunders opened his notebook and cleared his throat. 'One of the suspects admitted that his accomplice turned to the queue of people in the bank and told them there was a hold-up.'

'I only meant it was taking a long time,' Arnold protested.

'It probably looked worse because he was wearing a balaclava on his head,' I said.

'Why was that?' asked Sergeant McIntosh.

'Where else would I wear it?' asked Arnold.

'It was really cold,' I explained.

'OK,' Sergeant McIntosh said calmly. 'Saunders, I'd like you to wait for me in the interview room. I'll be there in ten minutes with more questions.'

The hope in my belly died like the embers of a fire and I went to follow Constable Saunders into the room. Sergeant McIntosh's hand on my shoulder stopped me in my tracks. 'Not you two,' she said with a smile and she closed the door, leaving the young policeman alone in the interview room.

'We're not being arrested?' I asked.

Sergeant McIntosh walked us back up the corridor towards the station desk. 'Why would two kids hand in a wallet containing hundreds of pounds in the morning then try and hold-up a bank in the afternoon? It just doesn't make sense. I can tell when kids are lying and when they're telling the truth.'

'We were going to come into the station and explain. Tomorrow.'

'Why not today?'

Arnold and I looked at each other. 'We were hoping to go to the rugby match with my family,' I said sadly, glancing at my watch. It was nearly quarter to three. 'But it's too late now.'

We reached the desk at the front of the station.

'Actually,' said Sergeant McIntosh, 'wait here one

second. The reason I asked you to come in was because I asked my brother to drop by and say hello.'

Even though all was lost I still had this powerful urge to hurry to the Square to see my family. 'That's really nice,' I said, 'but we'd really like to get going, if that's all right?'

Sergeant McIntosh's eyebrows made a straight line low over her eyes. 'My brother is a very busy man,' she said sternly. 'He's been here since two-fifteen waiting to speak to you two. He is in as much of a hurry as you are, believe you me. Now I am asking you to wait here – is that understood?'

Arnold and I nodded meekly and watched the sergeant bustle away.

While we waited I suggested Arnold ring the club shop and ask whether, by any chance, they were still holding the tickets for us. As we expected, the answer was no. The lady from the ticket office had just left to go to work in the hospitality suite. She had held onto our tickets until two-thirty but had eventually returned them to the ticket office. They had sold immediately.

I saw Sergeant McIntosh approaching, mostly obscuring the figure behind her.

'So these are the two boys I was telling you about. The ones hoping to go to the match today.' She stepped to one side and my mouth fell open.

'Pleased to meet you,' the man said, offering his hand to me.

'Owen Ritchie,' I said, shaking it vigorously.

'Why are you giving a false name?' Arnold whispered.

I laughed, finally letting the man's hand go. 'I don't mean *I'm* Owen Ritchie – he is.'

Arnold stared at the man. 'Owen Ritchie the famous rugby player?' he said.

'Guilty as charged,' Owen Ritchie laughed. 'Listen – Rosie tells me you're a mad keen Panthers fan?'

I nodded, grinning stupidly.

'Who's Rosie?' Arnold asked.

Owen Ritchie put his arm round Sergeant McIntosh. 'My big sister here.'

'Oi! Less of the *big* if you don't mind,' Sergeant McIntosh laughed.

'Owen Ritchie is your brother?' I laughed.

'Well, I did tell you he was a pretty good rugby player, did I not?'

'Talk about an understatement,' I gushed.

Owen Ritchie continued, 'Rosie told me you've had a rough year and that you'd done a good deed, handing in a wallet full of cash. She thought you deserved a reward ... Perhaps you'd like to come to a training session and meet the team some time?'

I couldn't believe Owen Ritchie was inviting me to

224

watch the Panthers train and meet the players. All I could think about was how Lenny would have been freaking out right now if he'd been here. I couldn't speak because of the lump in my throat so I kept grinning inanely.

Then Arnold said, 'And can you get us into the match today?'

'Arnold!' I said, sounding like a parent reprimanding a cheeky child.

'What?' Arnold retorted. Owen Ritchie smiled. 'As it happens I have five tickets in my wallet, just for you.'

'Are you serious?'

'Absolutely.' Owen Ritchie nodded. 'Rosie mentioned that the match today has a special significance to you. She asked me if there was any way I could get you in. I'm happy to help.'

'I don't know what to say. Thank you.' I gave Sergeant McIntosh a grateful smile.

'Och, don't mention it, laddie,' she said. 'I may look scary on the outside but I've got a soft centre. Talking of "soft," I'd better go and speak to Constable Saunders. I hope you all enjoy the match.'

Owen Ritchie checked his watch. 'Listen, boys, we'd better hurry – it's nearly kick-off time. Do you need a lift to the stadium?'

This was too surreal. Not only was my favourite rugby player in the whole world giving us tickets to the biggest match of the season, he was offering us a lift to the match as well. Lenny would seriously have been doing back flips at this point.

'No thanks,' I said. 'But is there any chance you could drop us in the Square?'

22

It was nearly three o'clock so the crowds that gather before matches had made their way inside the stadium, leaving the Square almost deserted. I saw my family immediately. They were standing near each other but weren't exactly together. My mum was on her phone – presumably calling Councillor Thomas to apologise for missing their meeting. Dad was awkwardly leaning against a railing, arms folded, and Olivia looked like she was making herself as small as possible. I got this strong feeling that this whole thing was a mistake. Ambushing my parents with my idea of starting afresh by doing the one thing that defined Lenny suddenly seemed like a crazy plan.

'Anywhere here is fine,' I said to Owen Ritchie.

He swung his Range Rover across to the curb and stopped.

'It was really nice to meet you,' I said, opening the passenger door.

'You too,' he said. 'And I'm serious about coming to meet the boys. Just call me.'

He had given me his number on the way over. We'd talked about his injury and he'd encouraged me to get back into rugby. (Arnold had given him a full rundown of my family's predicament, including Lenny's accident, my mum's overprotectiveness and my plan to get everyone together at the match today.)

'Nice to meet you, Mr Ritchie,' said Arnold, sliding out of the car.

The best rugby player in the whole world smiled kindly at me. 'Good luck – with everything today.'

'Thanks.' I smiled back then swung the car door closed.

I watched the Range Rover drive away until it was out of sight – partly because I couldn't quite believe that I'd actually met my favourite player. But also because I was dreading the reaction from my parents when I turned to face them.

When I couldn't delay it any longer I took a deep breath, spun round and smiled.

'Hi, everyone,' I said brightly.

All three of them were already looking at me as if they'd been watching since we'd pulled up. Olivia's expression was sympathetic – like she felt sorry for the wealth of trouble I'd got myself into. Mum looked furious and Dad's mouth was hanging slightly open.

'Leon Copeman,' Mum said sternly. 'You have no idea how much trouble you are in, young man.'

'I can explain,' I said.

'Do you have any idea how difficult it is to get an appointment to see a town councillor? How dare you trick me into missing that meeting.'

'I can explain, Mum. This is really important.'

'Important!' Mum sneered. 'What do you think is more important than road safety?'

I looked at the three people facing me and had to resist the urge to run over and hug them (it was pretty obvious Mum wasn't in the hugging mood.) 'Us,' I said.

Mum threw her hands up. 'Us, he says. Us! I've never heard anything so ridiculous.' Turning to my dad, she snapped, 'Haven't you got anything to say to your son?'

Dad's eyes flicked to my mum then back to me. He frowned and pointed at the curb behind me. 'Was that... Owen Ritchie?'

I smiled and nodded. 'He was so cool. He said I can go and meet the team some time. Can you imagine what Lenny would have said? He'd have been psyched.'

That might have been the first time my family had

heard me say my brother's name since his death. It was like I'd let off a landmine or something – the bombshell was followed by stunned silence all round.

Eventually Olivia broke the silence – her voice was calm and kind.

'Leon – why don't you tell Mum and Dad why you've asked us all to come here?'

'I've got us tickets,' I said. 'We're all going to the match. Just like last year.' I realised that hadn't come out right. 'I mean *not* just like last year. I just thought that we might remember Lenny...' I paused, struggling for the words to explain what I was trying to achieve.

Mum took the opportunity to launch. 'Remember? Remember!' Her voice was really quiet but full of anger and disbelief and maybe even blame. 'Do you think we need to go to a stupid rugby match to remember your brother? There isn't a minute of the day that goes by that I don't remember your brother.'

'I know, Mum.'

'So what is this about?'

She was upset – on the verge of tears. I had to explain myself clearly this time or it was over. 'Last year's match against the Kestrels was the last thing we did as a family – with Lenny. I thought this would be a good place for us to start ... over.'

'Start over?' Mum rolled her eyes and laughed one

of those laughs that means people think something is the opposite of funny. 'Just like that? You want to wipe the slate clean and forget the pain we're all feeling?'

Olivia tried to speak, 'I don't think that's what Leon's tryi—'

'Don't you stand up for him, Olivia,' Mum snapped. 'I can't think of anything more painful than going to that match today. Repeating the last happy memory we have of your brother as though we can just erase his memory.'

'Mum – please...'

My mum shook her head defiantly. 'I'm not going to that match. End of story. We're going home and when we get there you are going straight to your room, Leon Copeman. I can't even look at you right now.'

'Mum,' Olivia protested. 'Leon's trying to help.'

Mum sniffed and dabbed her eyes.

I hung my head and thought about the mess I'd made of this. It had seemed like the perfect way to get everyone together. All weekend I'd felt stupidly hopeful that this was the answer and now I'd made everything worse. If I could only find the words to express what I'd been trying to say. The thing was, every time I opened my mouth I made the situation ten times worse.

'It's not about the rugby.'

I turned to look at Arnold who I'd forgotten about

completely. He'd stepped forward to stand by my side and placed a hand on my shoulder as he spoke.

'Leon isn't trying to forget about Lenny. He wants to remember him. He wants to talk about him and do stuff Lenny enjoyed. He wants you all to feel comfortable talking about Lenny. He wants to celebrate everything Lenny was about. He wants you to stop avoiding each other and to start facing up to being a family of four.'

There was a moment of quiet. Mum, Dad and Olivia seemed to be processing Arnold's words. My sister was the first to speak.

'Hi,' she said, giving Arnold a welcoming smile. 'We sort of met earlier. Arnold, isn't it?'

Arnold nodded. 'I'm Leon's friend. I've been staying at your house this weekend.'

'Oh man,' I muttered. Having waited all weekend for the right time to break the news to my parents that Arnold was staying with us, I felt he could have picked his moment better.

Mum looked horrified. 'Our house?' she gasped.

Arnold nodded keenly. 'Your *cassoulet* was delicious, Mrs Copeman. It's nice to meet you again, Mr Copeman. And it's nice to meet you properly, Olivia. By the way I disagree with Leon – I don't think you look like you've been in an explosion at a hairspray factory at all.'

Olivia planted her hands on her hips and narrowed her eyes at me.

'Wow,' I said with a nervous laugh. 'And there I was thinking this couldn't get any more awkward, Arnold.'

'So,' Dad said, clapping his hands, 'if this isn't about the rugby, what is it about?'

'You never do anything together,' Arnold stated plainly.

'Don't be silly,' Mum countered but without conviction. 'Of course we do.'

Arnold shook his head. 'Leon says you don't even have meals together. He thinks you're afraid to do anything all together because that will highlight that Lenny is gone.'

'That's ridiculous,' Dad laughed. 'We do lots of stuff together.'

'Such as?' Arnold asked. I'd never have had the nerve to challenge my parents like this and I wanted to cheer.

Dad rolled his eyes up to the sky for a moment. 'The thing is I'm very busy at work,' he said at last.

'You're not at work now,' Arnold observed.

'Now?' Dad repeated.

'Yup. Why not give the rugby a try?'

Dad looked at Mum.

'What do you say?'

Mum shrugged and pursed her lips. 'I don't see how going to a rugby match is supposed to suddenly fix every-thing.'

'It's not going to suddenly fix it,' I said quietly. 'But it might *start* to.'

Mum scowled and crossed her arms.

'Please,' I urged. 'Can we at least try?'

'Well,' she said. 'I suppose I've already missed my meeting, haven't I?'

'Is that a *yes*?'

'It's a *I'm not happy about this at all*,' she said. 'But what have we got to lose?'

23

The first half was awful. An utter disaster. It started badly because we arrived at the stadium late and everyone huffed and puffed when they had to stand up to let us get to our seats. The Panthers played terribly and were losing by three tries inside the first fifteen minutes. But most of all it was awful because Lenny wasn't there. My notion that it was going to be a fitting way of commemorating him couldn't have been further from the truth. Every pass, every tackle, every song made me wish more than ever that my twin brother was still alive. It felt like his absence was bigger than ever and I hated every one of the forty minutes of the first half.

Owen Ritchie had given us corporate tickets – the posh ones businessmen use when they want to impress important clients. They included access to a private room at half-time with a sign on the door saying 'complimen-tary bar'.

'Does that mean everyone will tell us how nice we look?' Arnold asked as we filed in.

'It just means the drinks are free,' Olivia explained.

We found a table by a big window overlooking the pitch and sat down. Olivia stood and said, 'I'm just going to the loo. Back in a minute.'

When she left no one spoke.

A woman in a white blouse and black skirt approached the table.

'Hi guys, welcome to The Black Cats Suite. I'm Rachel – I'll be your waitress today,' she recited in a sing-songy voice. 'Are you ready to order drinks?' As she spoke she perched on the seat next to me.

'That seat's taken,' Arnold said.

The waitress giggled.

'Seriously,' Arnold said. 'She'll be back in sixty seconds so you can't sit there.'

'I'm only...' the waitress's mumbled explanation tailed off and she stood up, blushing.

Dad smiled kindly and said, 'I'll have a bottle of mineral water. Sparkling.'

'Ice and lemon?'

'Go on then. Let's push the boat out.'

Arnold and I ordered Coke and Mum said she and

Olivia would share Dad's water. The waitress returned a few minutes later with our drinks.

Everyone sipped. Silence settled heavily upon us. I wondered what Mum was most cross about – me cancelling her appointment with Councillor Thomas or me dragging her to the rugby match. My only consolation was that the first half of the match had been so uncomfortable, Mum had probably forgotten all about me smuggling Arnold into the house.

'Didn't you have any idea Leon had smuggled me into his room, Mrs Copeman?' Arnold piped up.

'I did think Leon was acting a bit strange,' Mum said. She sounded weary. 'That's why I was checking up on him so much.'

'You're always checking up on me,' I mumbled.

'Isn't that what mums are meant to do?'

I shook my head. 'Mums are supposed to spend time with their kids. Do fun stuff with them. Encourage them to have adventures, not act like the fun police.'

'What does that mean?'

'You're always telling me what I can't do. Who I can't invite round. Don't play rugby, no cricket in the garden, wear your helmet, don't cycle on the road. It's all you ever say to me.'

'Is it?' Mum asked quietly.

'Even when you ask me how school has been it's like

you're trying to find out if I've done anything risky so you can ban it.'

'I'm not that bad, am I?' Mum looked up at Dad, who raised his eyebrows apologetically.

'All I'm saying,' I continued, 'is that it would be brilliant if once in a while, instead of warning me about stuff not to do, you could suggest something we could do together.'

There was a long silence – like there is at church when the priest has said something meaningful. Mum pursed her lips and nodded. Her chin puckered up and her eyes were shiny. Olivia came back and slipped into her seat without a word.

'Maybe we should go,' Dad suggested eventually. 'We could get some ice cream on the way home. Do you like Ben and Jerry's, Arnold?'

'I don't know anyone called Ben or Jerry.'

'Well, do you like ice cream?'

'Who doesn't?' Arnold beamed.

'Then you're in for a treat. Ben and Jerry's ice cream is crazily tasty.' Dad pulled a zany face, twisting his mouth and going cross-eyed.

Arnold lurched forward, laughing and clutching a hand over his mouth as Coke frothed out of his nose.

'Jesus,' Olivia said. 'I don't know how you kept him hidden for two days, Leon. You could hear a laugh like that from the other side of town.'

I glanced nervously at my mum. I didn't want to upset her more by returning to the thorny issue of her checking up on me. But she smiled and said, 'I expect they just turned up the volume on the Xbox to drown out their laughter?'

'Something like that,' I replied gratefully.

Olivia broke the silence by recounting how she'd come home and found Arnold in the kitchen making toast.

'What did you think he was up to?' asked Dad.

'Well, obviously I thought he was a burglar,' my sister laughed.

'Sure,' Dad nodded. 'Those dreaded toast-stealing burglars are the worst, aren't they? Mind you, I have always wondered where all the good jam goes.'

'Don't joke,' Mum said. 'For all Olivia knew he was armed and dangerous.'

'Exactly,' Olivia exclaimed. 'It's funny now but at the time I was terrified. I really thought we were being robbed.'

'What did you do?' I asked.

'I ducked back out of the kitchen without him seeing me and called the police from the hall. I was whispering down the phone so Arnold couldn't hear me. The operator kept asking me to speak up and I was like, *I can't speak up because the burglar is in the next room.*'

'How long did the police take to come?' Dad asked, with more concern this time.

'Not long. About five minutes but after about three I started to worry that Arnold was going to escape. I decided the best thing would be to keep him where he was. So I quietly opened the front door and left it open for the police. Then I sneaked into the kitchen, grabbed the closest thing to a weapon I could find and told him to freeze.'

'What weapon did you choose?' asked Dad. 'A kitchen knife? A rolling pin?'

Olivia glanced at me, blushing slightly. 'Neither of those,' she said sheepishly. 'Actually it was a stick of French bread.'

'Nice choice,' Dad laughed. 'Who wouldn't be deterred from attacking you by the idea of being walloped with a crusty loaf?'

'So you saw all this happen, Leon?' Mum asked.

'I'd been upstairs for most of it,' I explained. 'I was listening to music with my headphones on so I didn't hear Olivia come home. I happened to come downstairs just as the policeman was trying to disarm Olivia.'

'The cheek!' Olivia continued, 'He looked all of about fifteen. The first thing he did was tell me to put down my weapon. I was like, *He's armed too.*'

'Arnold was holding a butter knife with menace,' I explained.

240

'Exactly,' Olivia agreed. 'But the policeman was all like, *Step away from the baguette.*'

'Guess what Olivia said to that?' I chipped in. '*It's a* ficelle *actually.*'

Dad groaned, rolling his eyes theatrically.

'Quite right too,' Mum said, smiling for the first time that day. 'A baguette is a completely different kettle of fish.'

'Why would you put fish in your kettle?' wondered Arnold and everyone laughed. Even Mum. She really laughed. Eventually she dabbed the corners of her eyes with a tissue, shaking her head.

'Oh, all my mascara's running,' she gasped. 'I haven't laughed this much since I don't know when.'

I liked seeing Mum so happy and didn't want it to stop. I mean, I knew she couldn't keep laughing for ever – that would be weird. I just didn't want her to stop just yet.

But she did stop because, out of the blue, Arnold made an announcement.

'Leon saved my life yesterday.'

It took me a moment to work out what he was talking about. I'd almost forgotten about our close shave with the bus at the crossing. Immediately I could see the stress and anxiety etching itself back into my mum's features. Instinctively I kicked Arnold under the table. A kick under the table is the universally acknowledged secret signal to someone to change the subject.

'Ow,' he yelped. 'What did you kick me for?'

'I didn't,' I said, doing the wide-eyed stare. The wide-eyed stare is the other secret signal to change the subject.

'Yes, you did. And why are you staring at me like a lunatic?'

'Where did Leon save your life, Arnold?' Mum's voice was icy calm.

'We were just crossing the road near Chambers Park.'

I could see Mum's grip on her glass tighten. Her lips went thin.

'I see,' she said. She was trying to sound interested but I could sense the fear in her voice. 'What happened?'

'It was nothing,' I said, waving a hand.

'Nothing?' Arnold rolled his eyes. 'If you hadn't been there that bus would have run me over for sure.'

'Did the bus jump the lights?' Mum asked urgently.

Arnold shook his head. 'The traffic lights were green. The crossing man was red.'

'Why on earth didn't you wait for the green man, Leon?' As she spoke she slammed her water glass onto the table. Her voice was sharp and loud. The bar went quiet.

'He did,' Arnold said. 'I wasn't paying attention and started crossing the road.'

'So Leon saw the bus and warned you?' Dad suggested.

'Well, he did call out.' Arnold slurped his Coke. 'But

242

the bus was really close and I sort of froze. Leon rushed in front of it and shoved me out of the way. It must have missed us by inches.'

'You could have been killed,' Mum said, more fearful than angry now. She put her arm round me and pulled me towards her. I rested my head on her shoulder and closed my eyes. Mum kissed the top of my head and said, 'I don't know what I'd do if I lost you too.'

I hadn't dwelt on how differently the incident with the bus might have turned out. Thinking about it now made me shiver.

There was an uncomfortable silence at the table. The light-hearted atmosphere of a few minutes ago had gone. It was as if that cheerfulness had just been a smokescreen masking what everyone was really thinking. Arnold's story about yesterday's near miss with the bus seemed to have blown away that smoke.

We all looked at one another. I tried to think what I might say to explain what I had hoped for from everyone being together. The longer the silence went on, the more awkward it felt. I wanted to talk about Lenny, but a year of avoiding talking about him was a hard habit to break. Mentioning Lenny might be awkward. Not mentioning him was excruciating. So nobody said anything. About Lenny, or anything else.

Except Arnold.

'So what was Lenny like then?' he asked loudly.

Mum breathed in sharply.

'I don't think now's the time...' Dad said calmly.

Fair enough. Arnold had tried to talk about Lenny and he'd been told (politely but firmly) not to. That was that.

'When is the time?' Arnold said.

'Excuse me?' Dad said.

'We don't talk about him because we find it too upsetting.' Mum's voice was firm.

That seemed to have put an end to the matter. Olivia studied her mobile phone. Arnold's head bowed slightly and he picked up his glass and swirled his Coke.

'Who finds it upsetting?' Arnold asked quietly.

'We all do.' Now Dad's voice was firm.

Arnold looked at me. This was my chance to speak up. This was the moment the whole weekend had been building up to – getting my family together to tell them I think we're falling apart because everyone's too scared to talk about anything.

I don't, I thought. *I love talking about him*.

It took a moment for me to realise that everyone was looking at me and that I'd actually said that out loud.

'Do you?' asked Olivia. She had a gleeful twinkle in her eye. 'Me too. I talk to my girlfriends about him all the time.'

'Why not with me?' I asked.

244

Olivia raised her eyebrows. 'I don't really know. I suppose I didn't want to upset you by bringing him up.'

'I love talking about him,' I said, laughing. 'I love going places he and I used to go to. I love remembering his wild ways and his cheeky smile. I miss him like crazy but not talking about him makes me miss him even more.'

Dad sighed and puffed his cheeks out. 'I try not to talk about him because I don't want to upset anyone.'

'And you avoid doing anything with Leon you used to do with both of them,' Olivia said. 'Which was everything.'

Dad looked at me and smiled guiltily. 'I'm sorry, Leon.'

'I was lucky to have a twin brother for twelve years,' I say, pausing to swallow a lump in my throat. 'Those twelve years of memories could keep me going through the saddest days but I'm scared they'll fade if we don't share them – keep them alive.'

'Why don't you talk about him, Leon?' Mum asked.

I thought carefully and said, 'Because I don't want to upset you. Because it doesn't feel like my place to be the one to say, "Hey, everyone, I really want us to start talking about Lenny".'

'What do you mean, *not your place*?' said Dad.

I laced my fingers together and twirled my thumbs. Shrugged.

Arnold spoke. 'Leon thinks what happened to Lenny was his fault.'

245

For someone so blunt he was amazingly perceptive. Just hearing the words brought tears to my eyes.

'You think it was your fault?' Mum's voice was a whisper.

Without facing her I shrugged.

'Leon, look at me.'

I turned my face slowly and said, 'I just think if I'd done *something* different that morning, Lenny might not have run into the road when he did. If we hadn't been playing chase, or if I hadn't stopped to tie my shoelace ...'

'You can't think about what ifs and if onlys.' Mum shook her head. 'You'll send yourself crazy. I know I do every day. *If only* I'd driven you to school instead of insisting we walk ... *If only* I'd told you to stop running around because you had a big rugby match that day ... *If only* we hadn't stopped at the postbox to post that letter ... If, if, if.'

'But I could have saved him, couldn't I?' I said. I felt a salty tear run into the corner of my mouth. 'I was right next to him. I heard the car. I could have grabbed him.'

Mum was shaking her head, black mascara tracks trickling down her cheeks.

'Yes, I could,' I said. 'I could have, Mum. You were there. You saw it happen. Lenny went into the road. I was right behind him, wasn't I? I could have saved him but I

246

didn't. I just clung onto you like a baby. I just watched him get run over.'

Mum let out a little sob. She held her hand to her mouth and took a breath.

'You *did* try to save him, Leon.'

I looked at my mother. It felt like my heart had stopped as I waited for her to say more.

'You saw the car and you screamed for your brother to look out. As you screamed you started to run into the road. You didn't even pause for a moment to consider your own safety. You just saw your brother in danger and you went to save him. I thought you'd both be run over so I grabbed you and pulled you back. I was clinging on to you to keep you safe.'

I felt an immense weight lifting off my shoulders. The guilt I'd carried since the accident just evaporated.

'So you don't blame me?' I whispered.

Mum shook her head. 'If anything I blame myself. I lie awake at night wondering what would have happened if I hadn't stopped you. Would you have saved your brother like you saved Arnold? Both of you might have survived to tell the tale.'

'Or would we have lost them both?' Dad said, squeezing Mum's hand across the table.

'I think that's why I'm so protective of you now,' Mum said. 'You're so brave and kind, Leon. I know if you saw someone in danger you'd try and help without considering your own safety. Just like you did yesterday. I couldn't cope with losing you too.'

'You won't,' I said. I put my arms round my mum and squeezed her tight.

After a long time we pulled apart. Mum and Olivia were crying, I was crying. Dad's cheeks were wet and even Arnold looked like he might have a tear in his eye.

None of us had noticed the waitress waiting at the end of our table.

She smiled awkwardly and said, 'Can I get anyone a refill?'

'No thanks,' said Dad. 'I think we're going to go.'

'Did somebody mention getting ice cream?' Mum said.

As we stood Dad said, 'Lenny used to love Ben and Jerry's, didn't he? He'd eat it by the bucket-load.'

I smiled. 'Yeah – he always used to call it Tom and Jerry's.'

I caught Mum's eye and for a moment I wasn't sure how she was going to react.

Then she nodded and said, 'I remember.'

24

The following morning we had breakfast in the kitchen – all of us sitting round the table together for the first time in almost a year. Dad had taken the day off work and Mum had postponed her road-safety meeting. We were all going to the cinema in the afternoon.

Everything felt new. I mean it all looked familiar – but it felt very different. The constant air of suspicion, misery and guilt was gone. It was as if Arnold had made us all face up to stuff instead of burying our feelings. It felt like everyone was feeling a little bit more hopeful.

Without Arnold's bluntness I might never have discovered that I had tried to save my brother. Maybe I'd always have believed Mum was constantly nagging me because she thought I'd caused Lenny's accident. And we might all have continued avoiding any mention of Lenny – allowing our memories of him and our family to wither away.

Talking about stuff had changed everything and I owed it all to Arnold.

Olivia went out to see some friends after breakfast and Mum made Arnold and me some more toast. While we ate, I watched Mum and Dad chatting in the hallway – even smiling. Then Dad reached out and pulled Mum gently towards him and gave her a kiss and I thought my heart was going to burst.

'Kissing's gross!' Arnold said, watching next to me. 'Fancy playing Xbox?'

Arnold and I were on our fourth game of FIFA when Dad came into my room. I could tell immediately from the look on his face that something had happened.

'Sorry to bother you boys,' he said in sort of official tone that suggested he wasn't really sorry at all. 'But I can't seem to find one of my watches and I wondered if either of you two has seen it?'

'What's it look like?' Arnold asked.

'It's gold with—'

'Your Rolex?' Arnold interrupted. 'I haven't seen it. Sorry.'

'Are you sure? Maybe one of you borrowed it and forgot to put it back?'

'Why are you looking at me?' Arnold asked.

'I'm not looking at you, Arnold,' said Dad. 'I mean I *am* looking at you but I'm not *"looking"* at you.'

'Sorry, Mr Copeman, but that doesn't make sense.'

'If you remember anything, I'll be downstairs.' Dad gave us a curt smile and left.

I breathed out loudly. There was a question in my head that I was desperate to ask but I knew it would upset Arnold if I did. I wrestled with the dilemma for a while. If there was anything I'd learned from Arnold it was that it was better to speak up if something was bugging me.

'Do you know where the watch is?' I asked.

'No.' Arnold casually shook his head. 'Shall we finish the match?'

'Arnold – this is serious. That watch is worth a small fortune.'

'How much is a small fortune?'

'That's not the point. Look, if you have accidentally borrowed it, please put it back.'

'How could I accidentally borrow your dad's watch?'

I shrugged. 'I don't know. But you did accidentally nearly rob a bank so you do have some history of this sort of thing.' I was trying to be light-hearted.

'Why does everybody think I took the watch?'

'Nobody is saying you took it.'

'Your dad seems to think I did.'

'He wasn't saying that,' I argued. 'He was just asking if we'd seen it, that's all.'

'He seemed to be asking me more than you.'

'That's not true.'

Arnold turned to face me. 'Do you think I took it?'

The mistake I made was pausing to consider my response. In that moment of hesitation Arnold had the answer he'd been expecting.

He shook his head sadly. 'Why won't you believe me?' His sad eyes looked into mine. Without blinking he spoke quietly. 'I didn't take the watch.'

I went downstairs alone. I'd asked Arnold to come with me but he'd refused so I'd left him sitting on my bed, arms wrapped round drawn-up knees. Mum and Dad were in the lounge. They stopped talking when I entered.

'Well?' Dad said.

'We don't know anything about your watch,' I said.

'I don't want to be heavy-handed about this,' Dad said. 'But I will have to contact the police if it isn't returned.'

I nodded. 'Maybe you should.'

'Look, Leon,' said Mum. 'I think we all know where the watch is – or at least who's taken it...'

'Do we, Mum? How do we know that?'

'Look, we don't know anything about this boy,' said Dad. 'He seems a nice kid but he could be a delinquent for all we know.'

I didn't know what a *delinquent* was but it didn't sound good so I said, 'Thanks for being so open-minded, Dad,' in a sarcastic tone.

Mum tried a more measured approach. 'I know you like Arnold and he does have some nice qualities – but he's been nothing but trouble since you sneaked him into this house. He's been a terrible influence on you. He's got you into all sorts of trouble. If he wasn't egging you on then none of this would have happened.'

'That's not true, Mum,' I argued. 'Arnold's been nothing but a good influence on me – on all of us. He's shown us that we need to talk about our feelings instead of bottling them up. He's made us see we need to pull together to get through this. That it's better to remember Lenny and celebrate him than pretend he was never here.

'I've had the best time with Arnold. I haven't had so much fun since we went on holiday to Spain and Lenny fell off the pedalo.'

Mum and Dad smiled fondly at the memory.

'OK, I've broken some rules and I expect to be punished for that. But Arnold and I have laughed and got

253

into scrapes and broken a window and given blankets to the homeless and accidentally tried to rob a bank and it's been brilliant. We've really bonded and he's taught me stuff – like how important it is to speak up.'

'Rob a bank?' said Mum, horrified.

'My point is that Arnold and I are friends,' I continued quickly. 'He's the best friend I've had since Lenny and I trust him completely. He's honest. Too honest sometimes. I don't think he could tell a proper lie if his life depended on it. If he says he didn't take the watch, he didn't take the watch.'

'Are you sure it's missing?' Mum asked Dad.

'Course I'm sure.'

'Why don't you have one more rummage around to be absolutely sure it's gone. Have a look in all the drawers.'

'I never put it in the drawers though.'

'Just go and have a look.'

Reluctantly Dad went upstairs and Mum and I waited for him to return.

'If it's not there we'd better report it missing,' she said.

'What's missing?' Olivia asked, standing in the lounge doorway.

'I didn't hear you come in, love,' said Mum. 'Have a nice time?'

Olivia smiled. 'It was cool.'

Just then Dad came down the stairs looking really embarrassed.

'Well?' Mum asked.

Dad held up his Rolex. 'I found it in the drawer of my bedside table.'

'What did I tell you?' Mum said crossly.

Dad shook his head. 'But I always put it on the top, not in the drawer. Did you put it in there?'

'Possibly,' Mum said defensively. 'I can't remember. I am the only one who seems to tidy up around here.'

'Why didn't you say so? Instead of letting me think it had been taken?'

'Well I assumed you'd have opened your eyes and had a good look around before accusing everybody.'

'I didn't accuse everybody,' Dad pleaded.

'No – just Arnold.'

Dad ran a hand over his face. 'I'm really sorry, Leon,' he said, blushing.

'Don't worry,' I said, jumping up. 'I'll go and get him so you can apologise to him yourself.'

'Oh, he's gone out,' said Olivia.

'Out?' I echoed.

'Yeah – it's like the opposite of in. I passed him on the drive when I got back. He was shooting off somewhere on your bike. Looked like he was in a hurry.'

A horrible feeling swept over me. Without a word, I dashed out of the front door, leaped down the stone steps and pelted along the drive.

25

I tried to imagine where Arnold might go. I thought back over the time we'd spent together and where he'd opened up to me most. One place stood out more than any other as being the one Arnold had connected with most. I clenched my fists and ran as fast as I could.

It took me twenty minutes to reach the pier. The sun was weak overhead but sweat was pouring off me as I dashed into the arcade. I dodged some kids and side-stepped an elderly couple as I weaved between the fruit machines, heading towards the far exit. Beyond the arcade I was on the wooden boardwalk of the pier itself. My lungs were scorched but I picked up my pace and sprinted.

Reaching the barrier at the end of the pier I came to a halt. My chest was heaving and I slumped over the railing, breathless and utterly dejected.

My bike was lying on the floor, one wheel spinning steadily in the stiff onshore wind. Next to it, lined up neatly side by side, were Arnold's tattered Converse trainers.

I thought about the conversation Arnold and I had sitting in this very spot after we'd won the jackpot on the fruit machine. He had opened up to me and trusted me with his darkest emotions. I knew how much he needed a good friend and I had let him down. I should never have doubted him and I feared he had reacted by doing something silly.

I leaned over the barrier, desperately searching the choppy sea far below.

'Arnold!' I yelled, but my voice was beaten back by the wind.

Again and again I called his name. If only I'd stood up for him from the start. When my dad had come into my bedroom I should have backed up Arnold without question.

'Arnold!' I screamed. In my heart I knew it was pointless. The sea was so vast he would have been swallowed up instantly. Every time I called his name I sounded more desperate. 'Arnold!'

It was no good. He was gone. I hung my head and listened to the wind whistling under the pier.

'Were you calling me?'

I spun round, startled.

Arnold was leaning on the barrier next to me.

'Arnold!' I laughed, barely able to believe my eyes. 'You're alive! I thought you'd ... you know.'

Arnold shook his head. 'What?'

'I thought you'd ... Never mind. Look, I'm sorry I didn't stand up for you ...'

'No sweat.' Arnold shook his head. 'I heard what you said to your parents. About me being your best friend and trusting me. It meant a lot. I know I've caused you some trouble this week and I wanted to pay you back for the broken window and Olivia's phone. So I went to the bank – with my cash card this time. I didn't have enough to cover everything but I took out all I have to give to you.'

'Honestly, you don't have to.'

'I'm glad you said that.' He laughed. 'Because when I came out of the bank I spent it all on these snazzy trainers in the sports shop next door.'

I looked down at Arnold's feet. He was wearing a pair of brand new Nike trainers – black with bright green flashes.

'When I heard you stand up for me I felt good – sort of worth something for the first time in ages. I don't know why that made me want to get new trainers.'

'I do.' I smiled.

'When Mum got sick I felt like it was my fault. I felt

pretty alone but you changed that. You've looked after me and risked your life for me and stood up for me. I'm lucky to have a true friend like you.'

Then Arnold stepped forward and did something I wasn't expecting. He hugged me, pulling me towards his chest and pressing his cheek against mine.

'Listen,' I mumbled, 'since we're friends, I ought to tell you I'm not comfortable with physical contact.'

I could feel Arnold's cheek squeeze into a smile and he said, 'Tough.'

26

My marker pen squeaked as I crossed out the date on my England rugby calendar. I still couldn't help counting the days, but now I was looking forward rather than back. One week to go.

It was Saturday morning, the last training session before the schools' rugby cup final and I was excited about playing. Mum had changed her mind about the dangers of my playing rugby. Or at least she had changed her mind about not allowing me to play rugby and other contact sports. I suspected she was still terrified something would happen to me but she was trying hard not to show it. I didn't know whether Olivia's words had struck a chord. Or it may have been our conversation at the rugby match that had made her reconsider. Either way she was doing her best to give me some freedom.

Hearing the doorbell, I bounced down the stairs.

I was expecting Ash and Tom to call for me on the way to training. I couldn't wait to play the sport I loved again. The prospect of being involved in the cup final next week was unbelievable. It was like part of me I thought was gone for ever had been given a new lease of life.

But when I opened the door I was surprised to see Mr Cheeseman standing on the doorstep. He was dressed in his usual tatty attire but there was something different about him. He seemed brighter, sprightly almost. And he'd combed his hair.

'Mr Cheeseman?' I said.

'All right, sunshine.' Mr Cheeseman winked.

'Listen,' I whispered, glancing over my shoulder. 'Mum and Dad are in so I can't...'

'Smashing,' he replied, stepping into the hallway. 'I must thank your mum for that *croque monsieur* – it was an absolute blinder.'

Mr Cheeseman was still confused about the meal Mum had prepared him when I'd brought him home all those months ago. Maybe the alcohol really had addled his memory but I thought it only fair to put him straight.

'*Boeuf bourguignon*,' I said gently.

'Sorry?'

'When I brought you home for tea, we had *boeuf bourguignon*.'

'Yes, I know,' he nodded. 'Delicious it was, too.'

262

'It's just that you said *croque monsieur*?'

'I know. That was equally delicious. As was the *cassoulet*, the *coq au vin* and ...'

'Mr Cheeseman,' I said softly. 'You've only been here for tea once.'

He smiled at me and blinked. 'I know that, you muppet. I'm not crazy.'

'Of course you're not,' I said, but I was thinking the opposite.

Mr Cheeseman continued. 'Every now and then your mother comes to see me at the bus depot. She brings me food and sits with me for a chinwag. She brought me a cracking *croque monsieur* last night. She told me about the effect your friend Arnold had on the family. Sounds like he really cleared the air?'

The image of Mum secretly taking care of Mr Cheeseman and Arnold helping our family made me smile.

'She persuaded me to get some professional help. I wasn't sure at first but then I thought about what you'd said to me. In the end I decided you were right. It's never too late to get my life back so here I am.'

I was still wondering what Mr Cheeseman was talking about when Dad came out of the kitchen.

'Mr Cheeseman,' he said, shaking the tramp's hand. 'How are you feeling?'

'Scared witless.'

'Don't worry. I'll be with you every step of the way.'

'Cheers.' Mr Cheeseman held up a bony thumb.

'Well, we'd better get going. The meeting starts at half-past.'

Dad escorted Mr Cheeseman onto the doorstep.

'Where are you going?' I asked.

Dad turned and smiled. 'We're going to a support group for alcoholics. I have offered to sponsor Mr Cheeseman's recovery.'

'That's amazing,' I said, feeling pride swell in my chest. As Dad and Mr Cheeseman disappeared from view, Ash and Tom turned into our driveway.

'Ready?' Ash called.

'Are you kidding?' boomed Tom. 'Leon was born ready.'

'Give me one sec,' I said.

I grabbed my sports bag and went into the kitchen. Mum was drinking coffee at the breakfast bar.

'I'm off,' I said.

'OK, sweetheart,' she said, looking up from her magazine.

'I just found out you've been taking care of Mr Cheeseman. Thank you.'

'Well, I felt guilty for kicking him out. It was the least I could do to make sure he had a decent meal once in a while.'

'I see where I get it from,' I said. 'Looking after people.'

Mum slipped an arm round my waist and squeezed me.

'Ash and Tom are outside so I'm going to shoot.'

'What time is Arnold coming over?' Mum asked.

'About one-ish,' I said. 'I'll be back by then. We're going to go out on our bikes, or something.'

'Dad and I were talking last night. Maybe Arnold could come and stay with us again soon. Maybe for a bit longer this time.'

'How long?'

Mum shrugged. 'We'll see. There's a spare room going to waste upstairs. It would be nice to see more of him – especially while his mum is getting better.'

'Thanks, Mum!'

Arnold had been to visit his mother a couple of times recently. He'd said she was feeling stronger and hoped she might be well enough to look after him again – some time.

I gave my mum a hug and kiss. 'See you later.'

When I reached the door she said my name. I stopped and turned back. With her coffee cup cradled in two hands, my mum gave me a sort of apologetic smile and said, 'Be careful.'

I felt an immense sense of love that made me beam.

'Don't worry,' I said. 'I will.'

WOULD THE **REAL** STANLEY CARROT PLEASE STAND UP?

ROB STEVENS

Stanley 'Carrot' has never fitted in. He's got bright ginger hair, he's not sporty like his adoptive family, and he's definitely not cool. For years he's waited to hear from his birth mother . . . and then, on his 13th birthday, a card arrives.

Stan wants to show his mum what she's been missing – but he's got a feeling he'd be more of a disappointment than a wonderkid. What he needs is a stand-in Stan, someone who is handsome, sporty and God's Gift to Mothers. Things are going to get seriously confusing.

Just who is the real Stanley Carrot?

'Touching and funny'
Julia Eccleshare,
Lovereading

9781783442287